JESSICA BECK

THE DONUT MYSTERIES, BOOK 33

CHERRY-FILLED CHARGES

The First Time Ever Published!

The 33rd Donut Mystery.

Jessica Beck is the *New York Times* Bestselling Author of the Donut Mysteries, the Classic Diner Mysteries, the Ghost Cat Cozy Mysteries, and the Cast Iron Cooking Mysteries.

For Emily, you are simply the best!

It's finally time for Barton Gleason's pop-up bistro, but the grand opening is marred when a fellow chef and rival from culinary school is murdered nearby in one of the staging areas. Suzanne stumbles across the body, and while Jake is away dealing with his own family issues, she and Grace tackle the job of tracking down the real killer before someone else's goose gets cooked.

CHAPTER 1

"SUZANNE, WOULD YOU MIND GRABBING more dishes from the donut shop?" Barton Gleason asked me as he tried to do four things at once in his temporary kitchen setup outside. His pop-up bistro was finally happening, and Emma and I were pitching in, as well as a few of Barton's other culinary friends and coworkers from the hospital.

"Happy to help," I said as I stowed the dirty plates in a cart, ready to take them back to Donut Hearts. Barton had decided to have his first trial run in the parking lot behind ReNEWed, Donut Hearts, and Patty Cakes. It was amazing what he and Emma had been able to do to the outdoor space, but then again, they'd been planning it for months. A hodgepodge of tables had been outfitted with quirky mismatched place settings, and the fire department had even loaned him the use of six dozen folding chairs. The bistro would be open only two nights, and then it would go away as though it had never been there at all.

Sharon Blake, my assistant's mother, was due to start washing dishes soon at the donut shop, so I knew I'd better hustle if I was going to get Barton his plates in time.

Wheeling the dirty dishes behind the scenes, I marveled at just how well it all had come together. I especially liked the twinkling Christmas lights they'd strung from a temporary arbor set up on the perimeter, giving the outdoor space a sense of walls that didn't confine the dining area. I was glad they'd chosen to do it in the evening. It was still warm, but the first hint of the cooler weather that was sure to come was in the air.

I parked the cart and grabbed the door handle to wheel it into Donut Hearts, but the rarely used back door wouldn't budge.

I hadn't locked it by accident, had I? No, the handle turned freely.

Then why wouldn't it open?

Something must be blocking it, but I couldn't imagine what it might be. No matter how hard I shoved, it wouldn't move an inch. Frustrated, I left the cart where it was and walked around to the front of the building. At least there was no trouble opening that door. I'd left it unlocked to allow the staff easy access in case they needed anything. Walking through the darkened dining area and into the kitchen, I flipped on the main light as I entered my daily workspace and looked to see what could be blocking the door.

In an instant, the happy occasion suddenly lost every bit of its joy for me.

There was a young man lying against the door, and what was worse, one of my kitchen knives was plunged into his back.

Was it possible that it was Barton Gleason? Even though I'd just seen him, the resemblance was striking, at least from my angle. It surely looked like him from where I stood, and I felt myself feeling sick with grief.

I rushed to the body, hoping and praying that I was wrong.

No matter who it was though, it appeared that the party was over.

I knelt down to check for a pulse even as I pulled out my cell phone. Dialing the chief's number with one hand, I tried in vain to find the faintest glimmer of life in the body. With a guilty sense of relief, I realized that it wasn't Barton after all as I recognized the murder victim.

That made it better, but only by a little. After all, a young man had still just died violently, and in my donut shop, no less. The body was still warm to the touch. I had a sinking feeling that I hadn't missed the murder by more than a few minutes. If I'd come just a tad earlier, there might have been two bodies waiting to be discovered there instead of just one.

The chief answered on the second ring. "Hey, Suzanne. I'm just finishing up some paperwork, but I'll be right over. I just told Grace the same thing. Don't you two ever talk?" He was clearly in a good mood, one that I was about to ruin.

"Chief, someone just killed Simon Reed in my kitchen," I said, doing my best to avoid the pool of blood seeping out of the body.

"Who is Simon Reed?" he asked. "Never mind that. Why would he be in the kitchen at your cottage? Did you invite him there? How well did you know him? I thought you were at the bistro with everyone else." After a brief pause, he asked, "Suzanne, is there something I need to know about?"

"No, it's nothing like that, Chief. I'm not talking about my kitchen at home. I'm at Donut Hearts. I brought some dirty dishes over here to be washed, and I found him. To answer your other questions, I never met the man until a couple of hours ago. I'll meet you at the front door. Call an ambulance, just in case I'm wrong."

"Don't touch anything else. I'll be there in less than a minute," the police chief said, and then he hung up.

I looked down at my jeans and saw a smudge of the young man's blood on one knee. I hadn't known him for more than a few hours, so he was mostly a blank page to me. Who would kill him, and why would they choose Donut Hearts as their crime scene? I had my phone out anyway, so out of habit more than anything else, I took a few photos of the body, the crime scene, and the surrounding kitchen work area while I was at it. After all, I never knew when a snapshot would be helpful later on. It was sad seeing someone barely out of his teens have his life snuffed out so soon. What would cause someone to do such a thing? I heard someone pounding at the front door, and I realized that I hadn't unlocked it as I'd promised. Even though it had been unlocked when I'd arrived, it was second nature for me to always lock that door behind me if I wasn't open for business, and evidently I'd done it again.

I opened the door to find the police chief and two EMTs waiting impatiently for me.

"Sorry about that," I said as I stepped aside before they ran me over. "He's back there."

I started to follow when the chief suggested, "Suzanne, why don't you sit out here for a minute? Should I call Jake for you?"

"He's in Raleigh," I said. "His nephew's in trouble again." Jake's sister, Sarah, had a bad history with the men in her life, always choosing the worst available option. Unfortunately, Jake's niece and nephew suffered from their mother's bad decisions, and Paul, a teenager full of hormones and angst, was acting out in a major way. Jake had asked for my blessing to go try to straighten him out, and I'd readily agreed.

"I'll call Grace, then," the chief said.

I didn't even fight him on it. The truth was that I didn't want to be alone.

My best friend came in three minutes later and offered me a hug before she even said a word. "I'm so sorry," she finally said. "It's never easy finding a body, is it?"

"Honestly, I'm kind of glad I'm not used to it," I said, feeling the shakes that often came after something traumatic happened. I usually kept my cool in the midst of a crisis, but when it was over, *that* was usually when I fell apart.

"Stephen told me it was a young man, but that was all that he said. It wasn't Barton, was it?"

I shook my head. "I thought so at first, but no, it was one of his friends helping out for the evening." I couldn't imagine how Emma would have taken it if her boyfriend had been the victim.

"Who would do such a thing?" she asked me.

"I have no idea," I admitted. "I saw Emma having words with Simon earlier, but there's no way it can be related to this."

"Words? Do you mean they were fighting?"

I knew I'd have to tell Chief Grant what I'd seen, but it made me feel like a traitor to my friend and lone employee to repeat it to Grace. "I'm sure it had nothing to do with this."

"Suzanne, I know you better than that. What happened? You can trust me. Surely you know that by now, after all that we've been through."

"Emma slapped his face," I said softly.

"What? Why would she do something like that? It doesn't sound like her."

"Grace, I wasn't spying on them or anything, but I saw him reach out and pat her rear as she walked past him. Emma reacted much the same way either one of us would have. There's another problem. I think Barton saw what happened too. He looked mad enough to spit fire."

"I thought you said this guy was his friend."

"Clearly he wasn't *that* good a friend, or he wouldn't have done what he did," I said. "I've got to tell the chief what I saw though, and the thought of doing it is killing me." It was a poor choice of words given the circumstances, but it was true enough.

The EMTs wheeled the body out past us, covered in a sheet. They must have put Simon on the gurney sideways, since the knife wasn't sticking straight up from the cover. I got up and held the door for them, and one of the EMTs actually thanked me. It was all much too polite and civilized for my taste, given the circumstances.

The chief walked out a few minutes later, and he headed straight for us. "Thanks for coming," he told Grace. "Would you mind waiting outside for a minute?"

Grace frowned at him, and then she looked at me. I nodded, and she reached out and patted my shoulder before she left.

The chief pulled out a little notebook and said, "Now tell me everything that happened."

I took a deep breath, and then I got started. "I was bringing in some dirty dishes for Sharon Blake to wash when she gets here in about half an hour, but I couldn't get the back door open. I had to walk around to the front, and when I came into my kitchen, I saw the body. At first I thought it was Barton, but when I checked for a pulse, I realized that it was his friend, thank goodness for small favors."

"You said his name was Simon Reed?" the chief asked. The use of the past tense and the way they'd removed his body both made it clear that the young man had been dead indeed when I'd found him, but it was still hard to take in.

"That's right. From what I understand, he was a friend of Barton's from culinary school helping out for the next two nights," I replied.

"Do you know *any* reason anyone would want to kill him?" the chief asked.

"No, I don't know why anyone would want to *kill* him," I said. That much was true. A pat on the fanny might have made Emma and Barton mad, but it wasn't a capital offense.

"But you know something, don't you?" the chief asked as he looked at me closely. "Suzanne, I can't do my job if you don't tell me everything you know."

There was no getting around it. I was going to have to come clean with what I'd witnessed. "Earlier, I saw Simon pat Emma's bottom, and she slapped him for it. Barton saw the entire thing, and he was pretty angry about the whole thing. Really, who can blame him?"

"When did this happen?"

"Less than half an hour ago," I admitted. "Chief, Barton and Emma are both just kids, and good ones at that. Neither one of them is a cold-blooded killer."

"There was nothing cold about the way that boy was stabbed in the back," the chief said. "It was clearly done on the spur of the moment. Am I missing my guess, or was the murder weapon one of your knives?"

"It's mine," I admitted, afraid that I wasn't helping my friends any with my admission. I'd had no problem recognizing it immediately, since I used it every day. Past tense. Even if I ever got it back, I would never use it again, not after what had happened.

"So it was probably a spontaneous reaction to *something*," the chief said. "What else do you know about young Mr. Reed?"

"Not much," I admitted. "You'll have to talk to Barton about him. They were friends."

"Oh, I plan to," he said as he looked around my workspace. "Don't worry about your kitchen. You should have it back in time to start making donuts in the morning."

I hadn't actually even thought about that. I glanced at the clock and saw that in less than seven hours, it would be time for me to make the donuts yet again. I wasn't all that happy about doing it in the aftermath of a crime scene, but I wasn't going to shut my shop down voluntarily, either. After all, I couldn't stop my world just because of what had happened, but that didn't mean that I was going to take it lying down, either. Whoever had killed Simon Reed had violated my space, my inner sanctum, and I was angry beyond words. I might not have known the young man well, but he'd become a part of my world simply because of the place where he'd been murdered. In some ways, it was really none of my business, but that wasn't the way I was taking it. It felt as though it was a direct slap in the face, a challenge daring me to catch whoever had done it on my home turf. I quickly realized that might be the only way I'd be able to erase the memory of what I'd just stumbled across and recapture the joy I felt about my donut shop again.

"Is that all you need from me?" I asked him as I stood.

"For now. Hang around, though. I might need more information later."

"You don't have to worry about me. I'm not going anywhere," I said as I headed for the door.

"Suzanne," he called out before I could escape.

"Yes?"

"I'm sorry you had to be the one who found the body," the chief said sympathetically.

"That makes two of us. Thanks, though," I replied.

"I'll see you soon," he answered, instantly dismissing me from his thoughts and already focusing on who might have stabbed the young man whose body I'd just literally stumbled upon. I wasn't sure that Chief Grant was going to like it, but he was about to have some company in his investigation, and if I could talk Grace into helping me, so much the better.

But either way, I was determined to find out who had killed Simon Reed in my donut shop.

CHAPTER 2

"How did Stephen react to the news?" Grace asked me the moment I joined her outside.

"Are you talking about me telling him what happened between Simon and Emma? I couldn't say. He's hard to read sometimes, isn't he?"

"You don't have to tell me. That's not what I'm referring to, though. I have a hunch I know exactly how he took that particular tidbit of information. I'm talking about the fact that we're going to investigate this case ourselves," she said calmly.

"Are we?" I asked her.

"Suzanne, you aren't losing your nerve, are you? Someone killed a man in your donut shop. Aren't you outraged?"

"Of course I am," I said, trying to keep my temper in check. "Grace, you realize that we can't snoop around into every murder that happens in April Springs, don't you?" I'd already come to the same conclusion that we were going to investigate the homicide, but it still surprised me a little to see that Grace felt the same way.

"Maybe not, but I don't see how we can ignore this one. Whether you like it or not, you're in this one up to your eyebrows. Not only is Emma going to be one of Stephen's main suspects, but the scene of the crime alone should be enough to get you involved."

"Don't you think I know that?" I asked her, trying to hold back my tears. The emotions stemming from finding Simon's body were welling up in me, and it was all I could do not to break down right then and there. There was also the added stress of knowing that my assistant, whether I liked it or not, was hip deep in trouble at the moment, and so was her boyfriend.

"Hey, take it easy," she said as she lightly stroked my shoulder. "We're on the same team, remember? If you don't want to dig into this, we don't have to."

"No, you're right. Of course you're right. I'd already reached the same conclusion myself. I just get so tired of dealing with bad guys sometimes, you know? When am I ever going to get some peace and quiet in my life?"

"Unless I miss my guess, it won't be until after this particular murderer is caught," she said. "Come on. We can do this. Between the two of us, there's *nothing* we can't handle, and I'll be there beside you every step of the way. It will be like old times, you know?"

"I can't tell you how much I appreciate that," I said, and then I gave my best friend a spontaneous hug. Though I was packing on at least fifteen more pounds than I should have been and Grace sported the same svelte figure she'd had since high school, embracing her gave me a great deal of comfort. Just knowing that she had my back, no matter what, was all that I really needed to get through this. "Okay," I said as I pulled away. "We're both on the same page, then. We dig into this until we find out what happened to Simon Reed, no matter who might have been involved in it. Thanks for the pep talk, Coach."

"No problem whatsoever. It's the least I can do. After all, you've given me enough of them over the years," she said with a smile. "I'm just glad I finally got the opportunity to return the favor. So, what's our first step, boss?"

"Don't call me boss. I'm not in charge," I said.

"I sincerely hope that's not true," Grace answered with a

grin. "Because if *I'm* running the show, our investigation is in serious trouble."

"You're more than capable of being in charge," I reminded her.

"That point is debatable, but why should we wreck a good thing? Whether you like it or not, you're good at this, and I have no desire to run things, so why don't we leave things just the way they stand? You come up with the game plan, the list of suspects, and a continuing and ever-changing strategy to catch the killer."

"If I'm doing all that, then what exactly are *you* going to be doing?" I asked her with a grin.

"Me? I'm here for inspiration, my odd perspective, and my ever-present charisma," she said in reply, matching my smile with one of her own.

"Don't forget the fact that you've also got my back in case things get dangerous."

"You'd better believe it. I just didn't know how to word it to make it sound cool. Bodyguard? No, that doesn't seem right. Second banana? I'm not all that fond of that term, either. Can you come up with anything better?"

"If we have to name your role, how about investigative associate?"

"No, that sounds too formal and structured. I'll take partner in crime, though."

I laughed, happy to have her in my life. Only Grace, not even Jake, could make me laugh at a time like this. My husband was wonderful in a great many ways, but only my best friend could make me giggle seemingly at will. "Okay, partner. Let's head back to the bistro and see if there's anyone there we can speak with about the newly deceased. I'm curious to see how the chief's people are handling the crowd. It can't be easy, given the circumstances."

"Who knows? We may just see a riot if we're lucky," Grace

answered with a grin as we walked between Donut Hearts and ReNEWed to see what was going on.

The back parking lot, or more accurately the pop-up bistro, at least for the next few moments, was cordoned off completely, with crime scene tape already stretched around the perimeter. Two officers were standing at the only gap in the tape, and the folks that had so recently been dining there were lined up single file, being released in an orderly manner that impressed me. We moved closer to the heart of the queue, and I watched them process Paige Hill, the owner of The Last Page bookstore across the street from my donut shop.

"Name?" the officer asked her as he held out his notebook.

"Darby, you bought a book from me yesterday on needlepoint. Are you telling me that you don't recognize me this evening?" Paige asked him.

"It was for my mother's birthday," the cop explained loudly, just to make sure that everyone within a two-mile radius heard his explanation.

"Sure it was," Paige said with a smile.

"I'm sorry, Paige," Darby said softly. "I'm just following orders. The chief's a real stickler on us doing things by the book."

Paige's expression eased up. "I'm the one who should be apologizing. I know you're just doing your job. For the record, my name is Paige Hill."

"Could we see some identification, please?" Darby asked, clearly expecting to be blasted again for making the request.

"Fine," Paige said as she flipped her wallet open, pulled out her driver's license, and started to hand it over.

"Just hold it up near your face, please," Darby instructed.

Paige sighed a little, but as she did as she'd been instructed,

Officer Bradley took a quick photo and then checked the digital camera to be sure that he'd gotten a good likeness.

"Is there anything else I can do for you gentlemen? My blood type is O positive, if that helps."

"No, that's it. You can go," Darby said, and then he added quietly, "Thanks, Paige."

"Thank you. I hope you catch whoever did it," she said. As Paige walked past us, she stopped and asked, "Hello, ladies. What are you two up to?"

I didn't want any of the chief's officers telling him about our amateur investigation prematurely, so I motioned for Paige to follow us until we could get a little space and, more importantly, privacy.

"Everybody seems to be telling me what to do all of a sudden," she said, almost sounding bemused. "Has the world gone mad?"

"I just don't want anyone overhearing our explanation of what we're doing," I said apologetically.

Her mouth crinkled into a frown for a moment. "Well, everyone in town probably just assumes the same thing that I do."

"What's that?" Grace asked.

"That you two are going to investigate that young man's murder," she admitted. "Why, am I wrong?"

"No, you're not," I said. "Paige, did you see anything out of the ordinary tonight?"

"Maybe," she said, biting her bottom lip for a moment. "I don't want to get anyone in trouble, though."

"I can appreciate that," I told her, "but a young man was murdered tonight, and if information you have might help name the killer, you need to tell us."

"But not the police?" she asked, one eyebrow arching.

"By all means tell them, too," I said.

"But there's no reason not to share it with us first, is there?" Grace asked with a grin.

"No, I suppose not," Paige replied. "Okay. I might as well tell you what I saw. That young man who died, Simon Reed, was arguing with a woman earlier."

That was old news. "He and Emma had a fight. We already know about that," I said.

"I'm not talking about Emma," Paige said, a curious expression on her face.

"What? Who was it?" I asked.

"That girl over there," Paige said as she discreetly pointed to a curvy young redhead who looked as though she'd been crying. Barton was comforting her, putting one arm around her shoulder and pulling their heads close together, as Emma stood a few paces back, clearly trying not to interfere but being handy if she was suddenly needed.

"That's Sherry West. I met her earlier. Did you happen to overhear what they were arguing about?" Grace asked.

"She said that she wasn't going to take it anymore, whatever that might have been, and then she gave him an ultimatum. Either he could pay her the attention she deserved and stop flirting so rapaciously, or she'd find someone else. She also added that he'd rue the day they'd met if he crossed her again, and believe me, she meant it."

"Did she really use the word 'rapaciously,' or was that your word choice?" Grace asked her.

"Believe me, it was all her. You don't hear that one every day. That's what she said, though. It means…"

"We know what it means," I said.

Grace nodded. "Not everyone might, though. I love it. I might have used the word 'insatiably' myself, but that works just as well."

"At least we know that the young lady isn't stupid," Paige said.

"No, but that doesn't mean that she still didn't do something rash," I said.

Paige looked startled by the statement. "Do you honestly think she might have done it?"

"We're just gathering information right now," I said. "Thanks for telling us what you overheard. You really should tell the police."

"I will," she said with a determined nod. "Would you both do me a favor?"

"Anything," I said, not really meaning that my promise would be without limit. There were only three people alive I could make that vow to: Jake, Momma, and Grace.

"Don't tell anyone what I said until I've had a chance to tell the police myself."

"Of course," I said. "If it helps, the chief was at the donut shop a minute ago when we left him."

Paige nodded her thanks, and after she was gone, Grace looked at me and whistled softly. "Imagine that. We might have an erudite killer on our hands this time."

"It's hard to say at this point. We both know that intelligence doesn't preclude someone from committing murder."

"Woowoo. Preclude. Now who's showing off her extensive vocabulary? I would have said stop myself, but to each her own." Grace was clearly goading me for a laugh.

"Shut up," I said good-naturedly. "Who's next?" I asked as I scanned the crowd milling about. If we stood there and picked them off one by one after being interviewed by the police, it wouldn't take the law enforcement officers long to realize what we were up to, but it was too convenient having our potential murderer served up to us on a platter to simply ignore the gift.

We looked over the crowd going through the gauntlet, and I was surprised to see Gabby Williams storming toward us.

What was wrong with her this time?

I had a hunch that in a minute, I was going to find out.

"Suzanne Hart, what a fine mess you've got me into again," Gabby said. It wouldn't have surprised me if I'd seen actual steam coming from her ears; she looked so upset.

"What are you talking about?" I asked her, though I understood exactly what she'd meant.

"This," she said as she angrily gestured around the scene, "is all your fault."

"Gabby, are you accusing me of murder?" I asked her, knowing full well, or at least hoping, that she wasn't saying anything of the sort.

"Of course not. Don't be a twit. But even you must admit that it wouldn't have happened here if you hadn't strong-armed me into allowing this fiasco to ever occur."

"Gabby, I doubt anyone has ever gotten you to do *anything* you didn't want to at any time in your life," I said.

My comment seemed to take her aback, and as she began to reload, I saw Van Rayburn quickly approach. The two had been dating for some time now, but it still struck me as odd seeing them together. "Gabby. Remember what the doctor said," he said gently as he neared us.

"Doctor? Is something wrong with you?" I asked her, suddenly concerned for my friend's health.

"Of course not. They earn their livings making us worry about things that don't matter," she said abruptly.

"High blood pressure is nothing to ignore," Van said. "Now try to calm down and breathe."

Instead of flying off the handle at him as I'd expected, Gabby nodded, seemed to take a moment, and then she took in a deep breath, held it for a few moments, and then slowly expelled it. She repeated this a few times until she seemed to be back to normal, at least for her. "Sorry about that, Suzanne. I shouldn't have yelled. I just can't believe this happened." As Gabby spoke, her words were indeed much calmer than they'd been when she'd first approached me with fire in her eyes. "I know you didn't cause this."

"Thanks. I appreciate that," I said hesitantly. Was that actually an apology? Wow, Van must be working miracles with her. "I truly am sorry this ever happened."

"It's not your fault, so don't blame yourself," she said, biting her lower lip in an effort not to attach more blame to me.

"Let's go," Van said, taking her hand in his. Gabby seemed to smile a little at his touch, and they walked off toward ReNEWed together.

"Did that actually happen, or was I having a hallucination just now?" Grace asked from behind me. She'd taken a few steps back when Gabby had approached, out of self-defense, no doubt, based on their history together.

"I saw it too, and I'm having a hard time believing it myself," I said.

"It just goes to show that an old dog *can* learn new tricks," Grace replied with a grin.

"I have an idea. Let's test your theory and go tell Gabby what you just said and then see how she reacts," I answered, smiling in return.

"No, thank you," she said.

The bemusement we both felt about the situation suddenly vanished as Emma Blake, my assistant at Donut Hearts and, more importantly, my dear friend, approached us, crying.

CHAPTER 3

"**S**UZANNE, GRACE, YOU'VE GOT TO do something!" It was hard to understand Emma's words through her sobs, and I wrapped her up in my arms to offer her what little comfort I could.

"Breathe, Emma," I said, giving her the same advice Van had recently given Gabby.

After several moments, she finally managed to calm herself. "Sorry."

"You don't have anything to apologize for," I said. "How can we help?"

Emma was clearly fighting back the tears as she said, "It's Barton. The chief just took him away for questioning! He didn't kill Simon! I know it!"

"Hang on," I said. "The chief really took him in?"

She nodded. "He said it was too hard to talk to him with everyone else standing around listening in," Emma said. "I wanted to go with him, but neither one of them would let me. I'm a grown woman. I deserve to be there."

I could appreciate the sentiment, but I knew there was no way the police chief could let her be present during that particular conversation. "I'm sure it's not nearly as bad as you're imagining right now," I said, trying my best to assure her.

"That's because you don't know what happened," she said meekly.

"We know that Simon made a pretty direct pass at you,

you slapped him, and Barton saw the whole thing," Grace said succinctly, if not tactfully. "Was there something else?"

"It wasn't nearly as lurid as all that," Emma answered. "I shouldn't have made such a big deal of it."

I took Emma's hands in mine and looked deep into her eyes. "Now you listen to me, young lady. You were assaulted by an unwelcome advance, plain and simple, and you retaliated. You did nothing wrong, okay? We would have reacted the same way you did, wouldn't we, Grace?"

"Well, personally I think he got off easy with a slap to the cheek," Grace said. "If it had been me, he would have left with a limp."

"Grace," I said softly, reminding her gently that Simon had been murdered, after all. I didn't approve of his behavior, but the punishment seemed severe for the crime, to say the least. He'd deserved the slap, and quite possibly more, but his action hadn't been grounds for homicide.

"Sorry. I just hate the type of guy that thinks it's all fun and games, and they can do whatever they want to without any ramifications for their actions."

"We get it," I said. It wasn't the right time for a lecture on polite social behavior, no matter how much I agreed with her. "Emma, does Barton have an attorney, or should we call someone for him?"

"His cousin is some hotshot lawyer in Asheville. I told him to call him, so he's covered."

"Good," I said.

Grace pulled her phone out as we were talking.

"Who are you calling?" Emma asked her.

"I want to see why Stephen pulled Barton in to the station," she said. After ten seconds, she hung up. "No luck. It went straight to voicemail."

"He probably knew you'd be calling about Barton," I said.

"What can I do?" Emma asked, nearly in tears again. The girl was falling apart on us, not that she didn't have good reason.

"There's really nothing much that you can do at this point," I said.

"Maybe not, but there's something you two can do. Suzanne, you and Grace need to figure out what really happened to Simon."

"We already know what happened," Grace reminded her.

"That's not what I meant. You have to find out who did it," she said.

"No matter what we might find?" I asked gently.

Emma turned on me as though I'd just slapped her. "Do you honestly think Barton did it?"

"At the moment, I don't think anything," I said, carefully weighing my words. "But what if we find something you aren't happy with knowing? It's important for you to know that once we start digging, we can't ignore the truth once we find it."

"Barton's not a killer," she said resolutely.

"He's not going to be the only suspect, you know," Grace added.

"Do you think *I* did it?" Emma asked her. She looked at Grace as though she didn't recognize her.

"Of course not, but what the chief thinks I cannot even begin to guess. Your parents could also be suspects, you know."

Clearly that particular thought hadn't even occurred to Emma yet, but it had crossed my mind as well.

"Why would my mother or father attack Simon Reed? That doesn't make any sense."

"Emma, your father has been known to act rashly in the past," I reminded her, "and who knows what could have happened if Sharon had confronted Simon about what he did to you?"

"What is *wrong* with you two?" Emma asked shrilly with a

pleading quality in her voice. "Why are you both acting this way?"

"We're just facing the facts," I said. "The question stands and bears repeating. Are you sure you want us digging into this, no matter what we might find?"

"I'm positive," she said after a few moments of reflection. "The truth is all that matters."

I just hoped Emma still believed that when this mess was all over. "Okay. We'll do what we can," I said, failing to mention that we'd already decided to look into the murder on our own anyway. "It's hard to tell how long Barton is going to be tied up with the chief. Would you mind taking a walk with us in the park and telling us what you know about Simon Reed?"

Emma looked as though she'd rather talk about invasive medical procedures, but she nodded reluctantly. "If it will help, I'll tell you everything I know, but I should warn you, it's not much."

"It may be more than you realize," I said as the three of us left the crowd and headed toward the park across the street so we could have a little privacy.

A few folks were strolling along Springs Drive, but one of the benches in the park was free, so we headed for that one.

Once we were settled, I told Emma, "Tell us about Simon."

"You mean... about what he did to me?" she asked in a mousy voice.

"That depends. Did he do anything besides grab you once?" I asked her.

"No, but wasn't that enough? You know, I thought he was a nice guy before he did that. Simon seemed so attentive. When he asked me questions, he really seemed to listen to my answers, do you know what I mean?"

"I know the general type," Grace said, pursing her lips for a moment. "What about his girlfriend? What can you tell us about her?"

"You mean Sherry? She's always seemed a little harsh to me. Nothing Simon did was ever good enough for her."

"That may be because he was so… ah… attentive to other girls," I suggested.

"Maybe," Emma answered. "She's really pretty, isn't she? I just love her hair, but she seems a little quick tempered to me."

"Maybe she's trying to live up to the redhead reputation," Grace suggested.

"Maybe. I tried being friendly with her a few times, but she shut down on me pretty quickly, so I just gave up. I noticed that she paid Barton a little too much attention last night, though."

"Let me guess," I said. "Did that start right after Simon started paying attention to you?"

"Yeah, pretty much. Why? Do you think they're connected?" Emma asked.

I didn't have the heart to tell her they were directly correlated to each other, but Grace obviously had no such compunctions. "Emma, I know you're young, but you've got to see that was her motivation. Simon was making her jealous, so she thought she'd turn the tables on him and go after Barton."

"I may be young, but I'm not stupid," Emma said with a frown. After a moment, she grinned. "Barton is kind of oblivious to women when they throw themselves at him, though."

I remembered when Ellie Nolan had bid on a lunch with Jake just to get close to Barton and how my husband had reported that Barton had been clueless about the woman's intentions. Emma was probably right in her assessment of her boyfriend's behavior. "How about the rest of the crew Barton brought in for the bistro's opening?" I asked.

"Let's see. Clint Harpold was working tonight; he's Simon's roommate. They all knew each other in culinary school, and

Shalimar Davis was here, too. She had a history with Simon, but I never got their full story. They all live in Union Square. As for the rest of the staff, Barton and I hired a few from the college, or they were helping out from the hospital staff. As far as I know, none of them had anything to do with Simon before tonight."

So, at least we had a working pool of suspects to begin with that didn't include Barton or Emma. One of them might have done it, given circumstances that were trying enough, but a failed romantic pass didn't qualify as such, at least not in my book. That also eliminated, to some extent, Emma's parents. Ray Blake was a hothead, but I doubted that he would kill anyone over his daughter's perceived honor, and the only way I could see Sharon stabbing the young man in the back was if he were threatening her daughter with immediate dire physical abuse or death. "Good. At least that gives us something to go on."

"You really don't think anyone in my family had anything to do with it, do you?" Emma asked us both, her gaze and tone of voice pleading with us.

I was about to tell her that I'd discounted the possibility when Grace spoke up. "Emma, we can't play favorites. Surely you can see that."

"I get it," she said resolutely. I thought for a moment she was going to cry again, but she managed to pull herself together. "Is there anything else I can do to help? Would you like to speak with my folks? They weren't even at the bistro yet. Maybe they can alibi each other."

If that was the case, I wasn't sure what good it would do either one of them, but then again, maybe they had outside, verifiable witnesses to their presence elsewhere when Simon Reed had been murdered. "We'll be sure to ask them when we see them," I said. I appreciated Grace stepping up and handling the tough questions with Emma. I thought of my assistant more as a daughter than as an employee, though I wasn't old enough for that to be true, but it still made it hard for me to question her.

Grace had no such compunctions. "Where are they right now?" she asked.

"I don't know, but I can call them. Give me one second." Emma pulled her phone out as she stood and walked over to a nearby clump of trees as she spoke to one of her parents.

"Thanks," I told Grace.

She smiled at me, the relief clear in her expression. "You're welcome, for whatever it is I did. I thought you'd be angry with me for taking such a hard line with Emma. I know how you feel about her."

"It needs to be done. I'm just not sure I can be the one who does it."

"That's just one more reason you have me around," Grace said as Emma approached us.

"They're on their way over," she said. "They should be here in two minutes."

That wasn't good. If they were that close to the donut shop, they had most likely been in the proximity of the murder half an hour before. Some of the crimes we'd investigated in the past had iffy timelines that we had to work hard at discerning, but from the time Simon disappeared to the time I'd found the body was probably a matter of minutes rather than hours.

"That fast?" Grace asked, reading my mind.

"You make that question sound as though it were a bad thing," Emma replied, and then she understood. Despite her youth, she was quicker on the uptake than Grace had given her credit for earlier. "I get it. If they were close by, then one of them could have done it. It didn't happen that way, Grace."

"I sincerely hope that you are right," Grace answered.

Emma looked at me for some kind of assurance that Grace

was off base with her assertion, but I couldn't give it to her. All I could do was shrug, which did nothing to ease her mind.

The husband and wife showed up together as promised, both of them clearly unhappy about something. Emma picked up on it immediately. "What's going on with you two?" she asked them before Grace or I could pose our first question.

"Your father was supposed to meet me at home so we could be at the opening of your boyfriend's café together, but he stood me up," Sharon said.

"I did no such thing," Ray protested.

"Oh, really?" Sharon asked. "Were you at the house half an hour ago as we'd planned? I must say, if you were there, you did a remarkable job of hiding, because I certainly couldn't find you."

"Sharon, I told you before, I'm sorry. I was up half the night chasing a story, and I fell asleep at my desk. It could have happened to anybody."

"I doubt that sincerely," Sharon said, and then she turned to Emma. "I'll get started on those dishes right away. I'm really sorry we're late. I hope Barton will understand."

"You don't know, do you?" Emma asked them in disbelief.

"Know what?" Ray asked, stepping in front of his wife. "What happened?"

"Someone stabbed one of the young men helping out in my donut shop," I said.

Ray looked at me as though he didn't believe me at first. "That's not very funny, Suzanne."

"I couldn't agree with you more," I said.

"Did this really happen, Emma?" Sharon asked. "Are you okay?"

"I'm fine," she said. "Why would you think otherwise?"

"I don't know. It's always a mother's first instinct to make sure her child is okay," Sharon said a little messily. At the moment, I wasn't sure I believed either Sharon or Ray. Could one of them be lying to their daughter and Grace and me as well? One thing was certain. They couldn't alibi each other for the time of death. They'd both admitted as much to us just moments before.

"Let's get you out of here," Sharon said as she tried to take her daughter's arm. "We need to get you home."

"I'm not going anywhere until the police let Barton go," Emma said stubbornly.

"Is there any evidence that he committed the crime?" Ray asked intently. It sounded more like he was being the newspaper owner and editor than a concerned father, which was no surprise to me, knowing the man as well as I did.

"No!" Emma said, clearly upset by the question. She turned to us. "Are we finished here?"

"For now," I said. "Thanks. You've been a big help."

"You're welcome," Emma said, and then she started off toward the jail on foot.

"Where do you think you are going, young lady?" Ray asked her in an authoritative voice.

"I'm going to be with my boyfriend," she said petulantly. Emma was reverting to her younger self, defiant and full of rebellion.

"Come back here this instant," Ray ordered.

Emma ignored him and kept walking.

"Ray, don't be such a twit," Sharon told her husband as she started after their daughter. "Emma. Wait for me."

Ray had no choice but to follow them both, but I could see the hurt and anger in his gaze as he rushed to catch up. Evidently he'd been expecting his daughter to do exactly as he said.

Emma clearly had other plans, though.

Once they were gone, Grace looked at me and said calmly, "We may not have had dinner, but at least we got a show. We can't rule any of them out, Suzanne. You know that, right?"

"Even Emma?" I asked her, already knowing the answer.

"Sorry, but yes, even Emma. We need to keep digging, though. If we get lucky, we'll find out who the real killer is before it drives their family apart."

"Let's get cracking then, shall we?" I asked as I started back to the parking lot to see if we could get some time with the young people my assistant had just named: Sherry West, Clint Harpold, and Shalimar Davis.

CHAPTER 4

W E DIDN'T EVEN MAKE IT back to the bistro setting before we stumbled upon our next suspect. Sherry West, Simon's girlfriend, nearly ran us over as she whipped around the building. She didn't even pause long enough to say she was sorry, which, on second thought, I doubt she was.

"Sherry," I said, my voice cracking in the night. "Sherry West. We need to talk."

Using her name certainly got the young redhead's attention. She stopped in her tracks and turned to look at Grace and me. "Do I know either one of you?"

"No. We're friends of Barton Gleason," I said.

She frowned at the news. "Okay, if you say so. I don't want to talk to anybody right now."

"We're both sorry for your loss," I said automatically. The truth was, the young woman didn't appear to have been crying recently. She looked angry more than anything else.

"You *were* dating Simon Reed, weren't you?" Grace asked her.

"So what if I was?"

Wow, this girl was really on the defensive.

"We just thought you might be crying, or at least a little distraught over what happened to him," Grace said, voicing my thoughts exactly.

Sherry got up in our faces. "I'll save my mourning and my tears for when they find out who killed him. Right now I'm just incensed. We had a fight, and before we could make up, someone killed him. Can you imagine how that makes me feel? I'll never be able to make things right with him again now." She looked as though she might start crying after all, but after she clenched her hands tightly together, I could hear her whisper, "No tears yet, Sherry. No tears. Be audacious."

It suddenly struck me that this angry young woman was doing her best to hold it together. It was probably the only way she had of being brave in the face of what happened. I decided to change tactics with her and try to be more conspiratorial than sympathetic. It felt like the right chord to me, anyway, and I often had nothing to rely on but my instincts. "If it helps, we're going to find his killer," I said confidently.

"The two of you?" She looked at us, each in turn, in disbelief. "Don't tell me you are in law enforcement."

"No, we're better than that," Grace said, getting into the spirit of things instantly. "You see, we have our own reason to hunt down Simon's murderer."

"What possible reason could you have to even care about a total stranger? Simon and Barton weren't really even all that close lately."

"The fact is, whoever killed him did it in my donut shop," I said, meeting her icy stare with one of my own. "What's more, I'm the one who found him. You'd better believe I've got a vested interest in solving his murder. The real question is whether you're going to help us, or if you are going to get in our way? If you're on our side, all well and good, but if you try to stop us, we're going to roll right over you if we have to in order to get to the truth." It was a calculated risk, but from what I'd seen of the woman, I sincerely believed that it was one worth taking. Grace glanced over at me, but I knew better than to break eye contact with Sherry. "So you tell us. Which is it going to be?"

"I want the killer found more than you do. What can I do?"

Excellent. My ploy had worked. Now it was just a matter of pressing her further. "You can start by telling us where you were during the half hour before Simon was murdered."

It was a direct question, and it caught her off guard. "I was on the floor serving customers," she said. "Where else would I be?"

"For the entire time?" Grace asked her.

Sherry seemed to think about it for a moment before answering. "Yes. No. Wait a second." Her frown deepened. "I left my phone in my car, so I stepped away for five minutes to retrieve it. I hate not having it on me all the time."

"Did anyone happen to go with you to get it?" I asked.

"No, I don't usually need a chaperone to walk to my car," she snapped. "Why do you ask? Do you think *I* did it?"

"Right now we're just gathering information," I said. I could tell that we were losing her, and I had to do something to stop it before she stormed off. This young lady apparently liked to cultivate the stereotype that redheads had tempers, and I could see her using it as an excuse for her fiery behavior. "You live in Union Square with the others who were working tonight, right?"

"Yes. Why does that matter?" Her walls were definitely coming up.

"Did you and Simon happen to live together?" Grace asked her.

"We talked about cohabitating, but in the end, it was just too complicated," Sherry said. What was she not telling us? I had a feeling that the prospect of living together had been more her idea than his, especially if everything we'd heard about the man so far was true. The last thing he'd want was his girlfriend being able to monitor his coming and going around the clock, since her constant presence would seriously curtail his extracurricular activities.

"Did he have any roommates?" I asked her.

"He and Clint Harpold shared a place. He's around here someplace," she said. "You'll know him when you see him. He's six foot five and weighs a hundred fifty pounds. Just look for a beanpole with blond hair, and you'll know that's him."

"Is he a waiter, too?" I asked her.

"Clint? No, he's too good for that, at least according to what he thinks. Simon, Barton, and Clint were rivals in culinary school, but he never really measured up to the other two. It used to drive him crazy."

"Was the rivalry that heated?" Grace asked.

"From what I've heard, it got pretty dicey at times," she said. "Do you think Clint might have done it?"

"It's too soon to say," I interjected quickly, repeating my standard answer. "If Clint and Simon were such rivals, why did they live together?"

"You know how it is. We're all young, broke, and just trying to get footholds in our careers. Poverty makes strange bedfellows."

"I know it's tough being a chef, but you can work anywhere you'd like to as a server, can't you?" I asked her.

"Listen, I'm not going to lug food around all of my life," she said. "I have dreams, too, you know."

"Such as?" Grace asked her.

"I'm an actress," Sherry said, as though it were the greatest declaration ever given.

"And you're living in Union Square?" Grace followed up. It was a fair question, since there wasn't much of what you could call theater around us. The closest thing was my ex-husband Max's plays with senior citizens at the community center, and Sherry was too young by several decades to participate in any of those productions.

"I'm saving to go to New York," she said.

"Got it," I replied. I wasn't about to take on career counseling for this woman. "Where do you live now?"

"At my folks' place. It's not like I'm still living at home, though. I have an apartment above the garage and everything, and I come and go as I see fit."

Wow, this woman was bristly. I didn't care if she lived in a hole in the backyard. All I cared about at the moment was finding Simon's killer.

"Do you know anyone who might want to hurt Simon?" I asked her.

"No. Everybody loved him," she said. I knew that wasn't true, but a great many people had trouble speaking ill of the dead. I hadn't been looking into the man's life very long and I'd already uncovered a handful of people who might want to see him gone, but clearly we weren't going to get any dirt about him from Sherry.

I was about to ask her a follow-up question when her cell phone rang. "Sorry, but I've got to take this. It's about an audition," she said, answering as she walked off. There were no good-byes, no waves, really no general acknowledgement that we'd even been talking.

As Sherry walked away, forgetting about us entirely, Grace said softly, "It was nice meeting you, too. Take care, and good luck with that acting career of yours. I'm sure we'll be in touch later." She looked at me and shook her head. "I know I need my phone to stay in touch with the world, but there are times I'd be just as happy if they'd never been invented."

"I know exactly what you mean," I said as I strolled toward the back parking lot.

"How much of what Sherry just said do we believe?" Grace asked me. "Personally, I'm not buying the delayed grief explanation. I get that she was angry, but that doesn't mean that she still can't cry. Her boyfriend is dead, for goodness' sake."

"I don't know what to think. Grace, you know as well as I do that different people handle their grief in different ways. Maybe she's telling us the truth."

"About Saint Simon, too?"

"No, we know better than that. I'm not sure how much help Sherry is going to be."

"Then we move on to someone who had less reason to deify the man," Grace said. "It sounds as though Clint Harpold will have a very different story to tell about his former roommate."

"At least he should be easy to identify," I said. "Sherry gave us a pretty clear description of him."

As we got back to the pop-up bistro, I saw that most of the folks who'd been patiently waiting earlier were already gone. While we'd been talking with Emma and Sherry, they must have made their way through the police gauntlet and headed to their cars without passing us.

Unfortunately, there wasn't a blond beanpole in sight.

"We must have missed him," I said as I scanned the crowd.

"That's okay. We'll track him down tomorrow," Grace said.

"Are you going to be able to take some time off to help me with the investigation?"

"I've got meetings all morning, but I'm free after eleven. I can meet you here when you close the shop." She glanced back at the rear of my building. "That is, if you're opening Donut Hearts tomorrow at all. Is Stephen going to be able to release it in time, or are you taking the day off?"

"You know me better than that. He promised me I'd have it back in time to start making donuts at three a.m.," I said as I glanced at my watch. Part of me wanted to head to Union Square at that very moment to track Clint Harpold and Shalimar Davis down, but I knew that I'd have to be up and at work in less than seven hours, and I needed at least that much sleep to function at all.

"Are you going to be okay being there so soon after a murder took place in your kitchen?" Grace asked me gently. "I could always come by and keep you company, if you'd like."

"Thanks for the offer, but I know your sleeping habits, and they don't include being awake at that time of early morning."

"If you're sure," she said.

"Positive, but you get bonus points for offering," I said with a smile.

"Okay, then. Are you heading home now? I'll walk with you if you are."

"That sounds good to me," I said. We left the parking lot where the bistro had once been, and as we walked past Donut Hearts, I glanced inside and saw three uniformed officers crawling all over the place. It was all I could do not to go in and start cleaning up after them, but that was going to have to wait until the shop had been released back to me.

After Grace peeled off to go inside her place, I walked the last few steps to the cottage I usually shared with my husband. Pulling out my phone, I decided to give him a call before I headed off to bed.

It went straight to voicemail, and I wondered what was keeping him from answering me. As soon as I heard the beep, I said as cheerfully as I could manage, "Hey there, stranger. Hope it's going well with you. We had a little excitement tonight, but everything's fine with me. I'll talk to you sometime tomorrow. I love you. Good night."

There would be time enough tomorrow to bring him up to date on what had happened at the donut shop earlier, and there was no reason to give him a moment's unrest until I could tell him about it live instead of in a message.

Once I was inside the cottage, I took a quick shower, toweled my hair, and put on my jammies. I was still hungry since I hadn't had a chance to eat, and there was a little chicken left over in the fridge, so I heated it up and had that as a bedtime meal. It would be way too early for most folks to go to bed, but then again, they didn't have to get up when I did, so I didn't feel at all bad about turning off the lights and curling up with a good book.

I probably read a page or two before I fell asleep, but before I knew it, my alarm clock was screaming at me, signaling that it was time to start another day in the land of donuts and murder.

I wasn't sure what the day would bring, but at least I knew what I'd be doing for the next eight hours.

If the police had finished up with my shop, anyway.

CHAPTER 5

"**G**OOD MORNING, SUNSHINE," JAKE SAID sleepily as I answered my phone. It was twenty till three, the time I got up every morning I worked at Donut Hearts.

"Please tell me you've at least been to sleep," I said.

"I managed to get a few hours in. I set my alarm so we could chat, and then I'm going back to bed," he said softly. "What was the excitement about that you mentioned?"

I knew better than to hide the truth from my husband. "Somebody stabbed one of Barton's friends last night during the pop-up bistro. I found the body in my kitchen."

"Suzanne, I'm so sorry. Are you okay?"

"It's never easy, but I can't let it stop me from working, you know?"

As a state police inspector, Jake had seen more than his share of dead bodies, but thankfully, they were still an anomaly to me. "Has the chief released the shop yet?" he asked.

"He told me I'd have it back in plenty of time," I assured him. Before Jake could make the offer, I quickly added, "There's no reason to cut your trip short. I've got everything covered here. How are things going there?"

"Trending toward the grim, but I'm working on it," he said with a sigh. I knew that he was extremely close to his sister and her kids, and it pained him greatly to know that any of them were in trouble.

"Is there anything I can do?"

He sighed heavily again. "The truth is that I'm not sure I'm doing any good myself."

"But you're not going to let that stop you from trying, are you?"

"No. I can't give up on Paul. He's a good kid, but he's starting to lose his way. I'm not going to let that happen if I have anything to say about it."

I could hear the heartbreak in his voice, and I felt bad I couldn't be there to comfort him. "I'll drop everything and drive to Raleigh this morning if it will do any good."

"As much as I appreciate the offer, I think you'd better stay right there," he replied. I didn't get along all that well with Jake's sister, Sarah. The truth was, she never really got over his first wife's death, and she seemed to resent me for trying to bring her brother some happiness in life. That was her problem though, not mine.

"Okay. I get it."

"Are you and Grace making any progress on the case yet?" he asked, and I could hear a bit of merriment in his tone that was most welcome after the sadness I'd heard just moments before.

"What makes you think we're investigating the murder?" I asked, trying not to smile as I said it. My husband knew me too well.

"Call it a hunch," he said.

"We're digging into it, at Emma's request, but we haven't had much time to investigate yet."

"Why would someone stab a young man to death?" Jake asked. "You know what? Forget I asked you that. I've got my hands full here, and I'm sure you and Grace don't need any advice from someone three hundred miles away."

"Guess again. I'll always listen to any advice you have to offer," I said.

"You just won't promise to take it though, will you?" he asked, smiling again with his voice.

"Don't ask questions you already know the answer to," I said with a laugh. "I've got to get to work, and you need your sleep. Touch base when you can."

"Right back at you," he said, and then we hung up.

The exchange hadn't lasted very long, but it had started my day off in the right direction, and I was glad that I'd married a man thoughtful enough to call me at what was for him the middle of the night. I found myself smiling as I got ready and headed to the donut shop, and not even the homicide the night before could completely ruin my mood.

It did still put a damper on it, though.

At least there wasn't any crime scene tape out in front of the shop, and there was no indication outside of what had happened there the night before. For all intents and purposes, it looked as though it was just like every other morning I opened Donut Hearts.

Then why were my hands shaking so badly as I tried to unlock the front door that my keys slipped from my fingers onto the sidewalk?

I knew what had happened, even if there was no physical evidence remaining.

There were plenty of mental images though, and I wondered if I should get Grace's employee, Ramona, to come cleanse the place with sage as she had once done for the bookstore. I had been a disbeliever at first, but by the time the ritual had been over, I'd felt a lightening in the air. Goodness knew my shop could use some cleansing after all that had happened to it over the years. I had an anniversary of my owning the shop coming up soon, so maybe I'd hire her to come wipe the mojo slate clean. After all, what could it hurt?

I flipped on the lights as I entered, turned on the coffee urn, and, after pausing at the kitchen door, made my way into my workspace. The next order of business was to turn the fryer on to give the oil a chance to heat up to the proper temperature. Once that was accomplished, I turned to look at where I'd found Simon Reed's body the evening before.

There was no chalk outline there. Not even a bloodstain remained, though he'd been stabbed in the back. From the evidence on my ruined jeans, I knew that at least some blood had escaped, but the police chief must have had someone clean the floor for me, because the space smelled of disinfectant and cleaner. That odor wouldn't last long. As soon as the first cake donut batter hit the oil, that would be the only pervasive smell in my kitchen, and while I wasn't thrilled with the permeating scent most days, today it would be a most welcome aroma. I started on my generic cake batter that was the base for nearly all of my cake donuts, and then I tried to think about what to make for the day. There were certain standard donuts I offered every day, but I left my menu with enough leeway to allow me to be creative when the occasion called for it. Today I decided to do something different. Though summer was beginning to fade, I'd been playing with the idea of making a new lemonade donut all season. I zested a few lemons, squeezed them of their juices, and then took out a few scoops of batter and set it aside. Doctoring the cake donut batter with juice and zest, I started to mix it all in together thoroughly, but where was my dough cutter? The wide and flat thin piece of steel with a hard plastic handle was missing from its usual spot. Had Emma been moving my tools again, despite my repeated requests to leave them where they were? I'd just have to manage without it until I could track the implement down. On a whim, I went through our candy drawer until I found lemon candies. I liked to claim that the drawer was there for my creations, but usually it just served as a cabinet to contain my sweet tooth when donuts just weren't enough. I crushed a handful of the candies and added half of it to the batter. Setting that aside, I made up my standard cake donut mixes after dividing the batter into separate bowls, including a new recipe of mine that involved not only maraschino cherries but the liquid from the jar they came in. Used bowls were adding up quickly, and I was happy that Emma would be in soon to start washing them up for me. As I loaded up the batter dropper again and again, rinsing it thoroughly between recipes, I watched as the rounds formed then bobbed to the surface of the hot oil. It was a process I never grew tired of, no matter how many times I watched it happen. Finally, it was time for the lemonade donuts. They dropped fine, and after flipping them, I pulled them out and glazed them with my standard sugar glaze. If I liked the results, I'd mix up some special lemon glaze, but this was an experiment of donuts, not glazes. In all, I dropped half a dozen rounds. Barely waiting for one to cool, I cut a small wedge out of one and tasted it. My lips immediately puckered! I'd have to dial back the juice for the next batch, or everyone who tasted one would leave the place whistling, whether they wanted to or not.

I heard the kitchen door open behind me and I held out another section of the same donut I'd just sampled myself. "Taste this and see what you think," I said.

"Okay, but we need to talk first," Sharon Blake said.

I turned around and stared at my assistant's mother for a moment before speaking. "Where's Emma? Is she sick?"

"No, but she couldn't bear to come in today. She's still at the house with Barton."

"When did the chief let him go?" I asked.

"He only spoke with him twenty minutes," Sharon explained. "As soon as he released Barton, he came straight to our place.

Emma apologizes for not calling you herself, but she didn't want to wake you. Will I do as a substitute, or would you rather I go home?"

"I'd love to have you work, if you're willing to be here," I said, gesturing to the pile of dishes waiting for her.

Sharon grinned for the first time since she'd come in. "I was hoping you'd say that." As she grabbed an apron, she added, "Emma's really distraught about what happened. Thank you for digging into this for her."

"I'm not just doing it for her," I said, my gaze going inadvertently to the spot where I'd found the body not all that long ago.

"I understand that, but she still appreciates it. We all do."

"Even your husband?" I asked wryly.

"I know Ray can come across as cold and abrupt at times, but underneath it all, he's got a soft heart."

I wasn't sure how far I'd have to dig down to find it, but I wasn't about to tell his wife that. "I'm happy to have you here."

I mixed the basic ingredients for the raised donuts, and then I covered the bowl to let them rest through their first proof. As I finished up, I looked at Sharon. "I don't know how you two operate when I'm not here, but Emma and I like to take a break outside about now."

"Oh, we do the exact same thing," Sharon said. "Give me a second and I'll be right with you."

I grabbed my timer and started out the front door. It was too much a ritual for me not to take a break at that stage, and I followed it, even when I was working alone. I was glad that Emma had sent Sharon along, though, especially this morning. There was no way I relished the idea of working at Donut Hearts alone so soon after someone had been murdered there.

I took my seat outside, and I was enjoying the gentle cool breeze when Sharon came out and joined me.

"You know, I just realized something. I've never had the chance to ask you about your travels," I said as she settled in.

"Ask away," Sharon said, no doubt prepared to recount various trips she'd taken over the years. That wasn't what I was the most curious about, though.

"What drives you to do it?" I asked.

She paused so long that I was afraid that I might have offended her, but after a few long moments, she said, "That's odd. No one's ever asked me that before."

"I'm sorry. If it's none of my business, feel free to ignore me."

"No, I'm happy to answer it. When I was a little girl, my dad used to travel for business. He was away from home a lot, but when he came back, he always regaled me with stories of his adventures on the road."

"He must have gone to some pretty magical places," I said.

"I suppose some people might think of the broken-down old towns he visited as magical," she said. "The truth is, they were just a series of decaying old cities from the Rust Belt that most folks were fighting to escape from. But wow, you should have heard his stories! I now know that he went out of his way to make his trips seem special to me to make up for his continued absences, but I found myself wishing for the experiences he shared with me. I'd beg him to take me along on his next adventure, and he always promised me that someday he would."

"Did you ever go with him?" I asked softly.

"Sadly, no. He died before we ever had the chance, and I swore to myself that someday, I'd take those travels myself. I've been to London, Paris, Dublin, Madrid, and Prague, but I've yet to find a place quite as magical as my father found on the road, not that I don't love every minute of it. Being out of my comfort zone touring the world is what I was meant to do."

"Ray doesn't share your love of travel though, does he?" I

knew it took an act of congress to get the newspaper editor out of town for an hour, let alone take an extended trip with his wife.

"No, he's a homebody. I used to resent it, but when I discovered an old friend from high school who was in the same boat as me, we started traveling together, and we've been having a blast doing it ever since." She lowered her voice, though no one was within half a mile of us as she added, "Don't tell anybody I said this, but I'm not even sure I'd let Ray come along with me now if he begged me! We have our April Springs time together, but when I'm traveling, it's an entirely different world out there for me." Sharon paused and then looked at me guiltily. "I love my husband. Please understand that. But I've grown to enjoy the interludes when we're apart. It makes me appreciate him that much more when I'm back home. Do you feel the same way about Jake? He's out of town again, isn't he?"

"He's on family business," I said, not wanting to give her any more explanation than that. "But you have to remember, we haven't been married all that long."

"I understand," she said. Sharon's tone became serious as she asked, "What do you make of the murder?"

"It's too soon to tell," I said, my standard response when asked that question.

"I'm not asking you to name your suspects," she said. "But do you think there's a chance Barton did it?" There was an air of desperation in her voice that I wanted to ease, but I couldn't do it, at least not in good conscience.

"Right now, I'm not ruling anyone out," I said as bluntly as I could.

"Not even me?" she asked, half joking.

All I would do was shrug in response.

"Suzanne, surely you don't think anyone in my family is capable of murder!"

It was time to change the subject. "Emma and I have a policy of not discussing my investigations," I said, not coldly but not exactly warmly, either. "Maybe we should do the same."

After a moment, Sharon stood as she said stiffly, "Understood." As she started back inside, I touched her arm lightly. "Hey. It's nothing personal."

"I disagree. It's *absolutely* personal."

Sharon walked back inside, and I stared at my timer. I had another three minutes to go until the dough needed my attention again, and I was in no hurry to rush back in. I'd offended Sharon, and I felt badly about it, but what was worse was that I couldn't do anything to ease the tension between us. I could probably have just agreed with her that I didn't think anyone in the Blake clan could have committed the murder, but I couldn't lie like that. Better that she be angry with me than for me to have to deal with what I considered a betrayal of the truth. I knew that it was a fine line I danced, but I just couldn't bring myself to cross it completely. I'd been straightforward with Emma, and I certainly owed her mother nothing less.

The timer went off much too quickly, and with some reluctance, I made my way back inside. Sharon and I exchanged nods, but I worked on my dough in silence, and she raced through the dishes as though she had somewhere more pressing that she had to be. Things went on like that for nearly an hour when I realized she was staring at me.

When I turned to face her, she said softly, "I'm sorry about before. Can you forgive me?"

"There's nothing to forgive," I said.

To my surprise, Sharon reached her arms out and hugged me. I hugged her back, and after a few moments, she pulled away. "Are we good, Suzanne?"

"As good as we can be," I said.

"Then can I have another taste of that lemonade cake donut?"

Her reaction the first time had told me everything that I'd needed to know. "You don't have to do it for me," I said with a smile. "I know how tart they are."

"I want to, though," she said.

"Suit yourself." I gestured. "Heck, I'll even join you." I cut another donut, thinking that maybe I'd gotten one earlier that had all of the juice concentrated in it.

I hadn't.

If anything, this one was even more potent than the one we'd tasted before.

"It'll certainly wake you up, won't it?" Sharon asked with laughter.

It was exactly what we both needed. The tension was broken, and the rest of our time working in the kitchen went perfectly.

Then the first customer of the day walked in shortly after I opened the front door promptly at six, and I wondered just how smart I'd been to come in and make donuts after all.

CHAPTER 6

"Hey, Chief," I said as the police chief for April Springs came into the shop. "What can I get you?"

"Some time with Jake would be nice," the chief said with a shrug. "But I know he's out of town. Are you mad at me, too?"

"What do you mean, too? Did you make somebody unhappy with you already? The sun's barely up."

"What can I say? I guess it's just a gift. Grace was not very happy with me for pulling Barton in last night, and she wasn't shy about telling me all about it."

"I get it. What choice did you have?" I asked him calmly.

Clearly he was surprised by my show of sympathy, but I'd meant it. He was in a jam with this murder. I was certain that he'd talked to Emma as well. In my opinion, it was better to get the first round of interviews over with. In the past when I'd been suspected of murder, part of the dread I'd felt was waiting for that initial tap on my shoulder. At least Barton, Emma, and anyone else the chief had spoken with knew where they stood.

"Thanks. I appreciate that," he said, clearly relieved to see that I wasn't in a combative mood, too.

"You're most welcome. Before you ask me for my alibi, let me volunteer it. I was in plain view of two dozen people until I entered the donut shop, but I suppose it's possible that I stabbed Simon first, and then I called you. It would be a cold-blooded act doing it that way, though, and the crime was anything but premeditated, from the look of it. Still, knowing that you might jump to that conclusion yourself, I could have planned it to look like a spur-of-the-moment act, using the impulsive nature of the crime as a smokescreen for my wickedly calculated homicide."

Chief Grant shook his head in disbelief. "Wow, that was quite a speech. How long have you been planning your confession?"

"It wasn't a confession. I was merely stating the obvious. I found the body. Of course I should be on your list of suspects."

"Did you have a motive to kill that young man?" the chief asked. I had to wonder how much older he was than the murder victim, but I knew without a doubt that the job of our police chief had aged him since he'd taken the helm.

"No, I'd never met him until last night. I happened to see him pat Emma's rear though, as I already told you, but it didn't fill me with so much outrage that I thought he needed to die, however badly he needed a lesson in civility and good manners. I thought Emma's slap was a step in the right direction, though Grace felt it didn't go far enough."

"Trust me, I've already heard her opinion on the matter. If it helps, I don't suspect you of murder. You had the opportunity and means, but unless I learn something new in my investigation, you had no real motive."

"It's good to hear that you feel that way, Chief," I said. "Have you managed to come up with any new suspects yourself? I mean besides Barton, Emma, Ray, and Sharon Blake."

"Don't you get started on me, too, Suzanne," Chief Grant said wearily.

"I wasn't castigating you, I was simply asking you a question," I said.

"There are a few folks on my list," he admitted.

When he didn't reveal their exact names, I provided the ones I'd learned. After all, in many ways, we were on the same team. We both wanted to catch Simon Reed's killer, no matter what our motives might be. "Grace and I spoke with Sherry West last night."

"She's quite a handful, isn't she?" the chief asked. "I'm not sure if she struts that temper of hers around because she's really like that, or she feels she owes it to redheads everywhere. Either way, I wouldn't cross her."

"Which Simon evidently did with some frequency," I said. "When we spoke to her though, she was more than happy to point her finger at a few other folks in Simon's life."

"For instance?" the chief asked as he pretended to study my donut offerings for the day. The lemonade donuts hadn't made the cut, at least not in their current state. I'd have to tweak that particular recipe quite a bit if I was going to offer it to my customers, but I had plenty of cherry ones to fill the gap.

"As soon as I shut the donut shop down for the day, we're planning on speaking with Clint Harpold, his roommate," I said.

"That's where I'm headed this morning, so at least I'll get to him first." He glanced toward the kitchen and asked softly, "Is Emma upset with me?"

"I couldn't say. She didn't come into work today," I said.

"Suzanne, you said it yourself. I was just doing my job. Are you handling things here all on your own?"

"No, her mother is subbing for her," I explained.

"That's even worse," he said with a frown.

"How is that worse?"

"Emma yelled at me when I interviewed her, but Sharon acted as though she were disappointed in me more than anything else. I've known that woman for years, and I've always been fond of her. You should have seen the way she looked at me."

"Like you stole her dog?" I suggested.

"Yeah, that about sums it up. Did you happen to get any more names from Sherry? I heard you were lingering near the exit line last night."

"Which one of our troops informed on me?" I asked him. It might be nice to know if it was Darby or Rick I had to watch my step around.

The police chief ignored the question, and I really couldn't blame him. After all, I protected my sources whenever I could, too. How much more of an obligation must he have felt with his own people? The chief might have been younger than me, but he was certainly serious about his job. After a moment, he looked at me and asked, "Was there anyone else?"

"Not yet, but the day is young," I said. "Is there anyone on *your* list I've missed?"

He looked around and confirmed that the donut shop was empty. "Has the name Shalimar Davis come up in conversation?"

"Rats," I said.

"Where?" the chief asked, looking around the room.

"You know I don't mean that literally. Sherry mentioned her, too, but I forgot all about her. I'm so sorry. I swear I wasn't intentionally holding out on you."

"It's fine," Chief Grant said, taking it better than I would have if I were in his position. "Once you meet her, you won't ever be able to forget her again. The young lady is memorable. Yes, I suppose that's as good a way to describe her as any. I'm curious to see what you and Grace make of her, so be sure and let me know."

"Have you had any luck with the physical evidence?" I asked him, knowing full well that I was pushing my luck by even asking him the question. Still, if a girl didn't even try every now and then, where would she be?

"No. The handle of the knife had been wiped clean, and the only prints in back were yours, Emma's, Sharon's, and Jake's."

"You actually had our prints on file to compare them to?" I asked. I wasn't sure why I was all that surprised by the information, but that didn't mean that I had to like it, either.

"Jake's are in the system because of his career. The rest of yours have turned up in investigations in the past."

"Even Sharon's?" I asked.

"Do I really have to remind you that this wasn't the first murder that's happened here?" he asked me gently.

Too many bad memories came flashing back, and whether it was healthy or not, I did my best to suppress them. After all, what good would it do for me to dwell on such a tumultuous past? I'd rather focus on the good things that had happened at Donut Hearts over the years. "No, we're good. I'm really sorry about that slip. I wish I could say that it won't happen again, but I can't promise you anything."

"Even if you did, I wouldn't hold you to it," he said with a weary smile. After another glance at the display case, he pulled out his wallet and said, "I'd love two of those cherry-filled donuts and a coffee, to go. Strike that, I've been drinking the stuff all night. Do you happen to have any chocolate milk?"

"I do," I said, trying not to show my amusement that our police chief ordered like a twelve-year-old boy.

After I took his money and made his change, I said, "You know that you're entitled to a free treat every now and then, right?"

"Thanks, but I'll keep paying," he replied.

"I figured as much, but I still thought I'd at least offer."

"It's much appreciated," he said, and then, with his treats secured in one hand, he left the shop.

Sharon came out almost immediately afterward.

"Is he gone?" she asked as she peered out the front window.

"Yes. Why, did you want to talk to him? I'm sure I can still catch him if I hurry," I said as I headed for the door.

She gripped my arm tightly. "No! Don't do that!"

"Okay," I said, freeing myself. "I won't. Why are you so jumpy?"

"I thought he was coming here to arrest me," Sharon said, the fear alive in her gaze.

"Why would he do that? You didn't kill Simon Reed, did you?" I asked her.

"What? No! Of course not!"

"Then why would he arrest you for the man's murder?"

"I don't know. People get arrested all of the time for things they didn't do," she explained.

"I don't think you'll have to worry about our chief," I said. "I can't imagine him charging anyone without having a ton of evidence against them first. Take a deep breath, okay?"

She nodded and did as I'd suggested literally.

"Did that help?" I asked her.

"It kind of did." As she looked around the room, she asked, "Don't we have any customers?"

"None at the moment, but it's still early. I should push my opening back to seven just to teach them a lesson. If I did that, I could sleep in until four a.m. every day."

"Could you do that, though?" she asked me.

"It's my shop. That's the beauty of it. I can do whatever I want."

"I know that. I'm just asking if you could actually force yourself to sleep in? I know I couldn't. Getting up early is a hard habit to break, isn't it?"

"Tell me about it. If you ever figure out how to do it, be sure to let me know."

As I said it, three men in full hiking regalia covered in dirt and grime came into the donut shop. We were nowhere near the Appalachian Trail, but they looked as though they could have just stepped off it. "Gentlemen, excuse me for saying so, but you look as though you've all been ridden hard and put up wet."

They loved the comment, and I let out a small sigh. Sometimes my humor and my word choices got me into trouble, but I'd read their smiles as them being delighted to be there, and they hadn't disappointed me.

The older one of the group explained, "We've been hiking for three days, and let me say, your sign was a wondrous image to behold." He took a deep breath and exhaled slowly. "If you could bottle that, you'd make a fortune."

"The thought has crossed my mind before," I said with a smile. "What can I get you gentlemen?"

"Has anyone ever come in and ordered one of each donut on the menu?" one of the men asked.

"Not to eat on the spot, no," I admitted.

"Then we shall be the first," the third one declared, taking out his wallet and sliding a credit card across the counter to me. "One of each, please, plus three cups of coffee, and three glasses of water as well."

"Sounds good to me," I said as I rang up the order. I had quite a selection of donuts, but there weren't as many as some folks might have realized. After all, the glazed yeast donuts were a good half of my offerings alone, though there were several on the menu that sported different toppings.

It took four trays, and that was with some stacking. I started delivering them to my largest table, and the men dove into my donuts with such gusto that I was afraid to get between any one of them and their next bite. To my amazement, in record time, all of the donuts were gone, their coffee cups had been emptied more than once, and the three looked as though they could go again.

"That was, without exception, the best meal of my life," the one who'd paid said. As they stood and started to leave, he stuffed a hundred-dollar bill into the tip jar.

"That's way too much," I protested. "Your donuts didn't even cost that much."

"Nonsense. It was worth every dime."

"Let him do it," one of the other men said. "We're out celebrating. He just sold his business for eighteen million dollars. He can afford that kind of tip all day long."

"Not if you three keep eating like you are," I said with a smile.

He wouldn't take the tip back, and I shrugged as they left. After all, it was his money to do with as he chose. Who was I to discourage his generosity?

Sharon came up and cleaned the table but not before asking, "Did they really eat it all?"

"See for yourself," I said. I dug into the jar and pulled out the large bill. "Here you go. This is for you."

"What is this? I can't accept this," she said, clearly flustered by the size of the gratuity.

"Well, I'm not going to take it. I don't do tips, since I own the place. If it makes you feel better, split it with Emma when you get home."

She clearly liked that suggestion. "I can do better than that. I'm going to give it *all* to her."

"Suit yourself," I said. "I just don't want to leave it in the jar."

"Are you worried about someone stealing it?" Sharon asked.

"No, I just don't want to give the change and the ones already in there an inferiority complex," I said with a smile.

CHAPTER 7

"GOOD MORNING, MR. MAYOR," I said when George Morris walked in a little after eight a.m. "Getting a late start today?" The mayor was usually an early riser, so coming in much after I opened was uncharacteristic for him.

"I was up all night talking," he said with a groan.

"Woman problems?" I asked him sweetly. "Is your attorney giving you fits?" George had been dating an attorney from Newton named Cassandra Lane recently, though I'd never met her. In fact, she'd been a secret until not that long ago.

"You might say that," George said glumly.

My heart suddenly went out to the mayor. "I was just teasing you. What happened? Did she break up with you?"

George looked startled. "No, of course not. Why would you think such a thing?"

"I don't know. You look pretty upset," I said.

"It's the opposite, actually. She thinks we should get married. She just accepted a partnership in a law firm in Charlotte, and she wants to make a fresh start there with me." He said it as though he were pronouncing his own death sentence.

"What in the world is a high-powered attorney going to do in April Springs? Surely she's not going to commute all the way to Charlotte every day. That would be brutal."

"Suzanne, she wants me to resign and move down there!"

I was shocked to hear the news. George Morris was a fixture

in our little town, and in not a small way part of what held us all together. "You're not actually thinking about doing it, are you?"

"Why shouldn't I? I've served this town for years. Don't I deserve a life of my own?" He was angry now, but I had a feeling it wasn't really aimed toward me.

"Of course you do," I said calmly, trying to bring his decibel level down, at least a little. "I just thought you were happy here. Could you live in a place as big as Charlotte?"

"If I had the right reason, I could live just about anywhere," he admitted. "No offense. I'm not saying I wouldn't miss you and Jake if I left."

"None taken. We'd miss you, too, but in the end, you're right. You have to do what's best for you. What are you going to do?"

"I honestly don't have a clue," he said. "Do you have any advice for me?"

Wow, it was truly dire if he was asking me for my opinion! "Just don't make any snap decisions," I said. "I'd hate for you to resign, spend a week in Charlotte, and then want to come back." That triggered a thought in my mind. "Do you really want my advice, or were you just being polite?"

"You know me better than that. I don't do things out of politeness."

"Maybe not in the past, but you've softened up some since you've become mayor, and don't try to deny it."

George took a moment before he responded, another sure sign that he'd grown into his job. "Okay, but not with my friends, and you're just about the best friend I've got around here. Let's hear your advice."

"You have some accumulated vacation time coming to you, don't you?" I knew that the mayor rarely used his time off, so it was a safe question to ask.

"Sure. Why? Did you want to take a trip with me?" he asked,

grinning for the first time since he'd come into Donut Hearts that morning.

"No, but if I were you, I'd take a week or two off and go down to Charlotte. Get the feel of what it would be like living there. If you need a place to stay, I've got a friend I could call." It was as polite a way as I could think of to ask him if Cassandra would mind having him stay with her.

"Thanks, but I'm sure that won't be necessary. Should I ask Cassandra to take the week off, too?"

I shook my head. "That would ruin the purpose of the exercise. She's not planning to retire anytime soon, is she?"

"No, that never came up," George said with a frown.

"So let her continue going to work. Make this test as real a taste of what your life will be like as you can, and that means she goes off to work every day and you fend for yourself while she's gone. What do you think?"

"I think it makes too much sense to have come from a donut maker," George said with a real smile.

"I'll take that as a compliment," I said.

"You should, because that's how I meant it. Tell you what. Give me two old-fashioned cake donuts, a blueberry glazed, and a cherry-filled donut, too."

"Are you going to eat them all here, or should I bag them up for you?" I asked him with a smile of my own.

"I'll take them to go. Thanks."

He handed me his money, and I made change for him, which he dropped into the tip jar. It was quite a bit less than the tip we'd gotten earlier, but it was still a nice amount. "That's some good advice you gave me, Suzanne."

"Are you going to take it though? That's the real question."

He pulled out his cell phone and grinned at me. "Sorry, but I don't have time to talk. I'm calling my girlfriend to see if she'd like my company next week."

"Good for you, and good luck. You know I just want what's best for you," I said.

"I know that, and I greatly appreciate it," he replied.

"Is the coast clear?" Barton Gleason asked as he popped his head through the shop door moments after the mayor left.

"I thought you were with Emma," I said, evidently a little too loudly for his taste.

"Quiet! I don't want Sharon to know that I'm here," he said. "Emma fell asleep on the couch, so I came down here to help if I can. Thanks for digging into what happened to Simon, Suzanne. You're a good friend."

"We can't make any promises, but Grace and I are going to do the best we can. Barton, were you in plain sight during the thirty minutes before I found the body?"

"No," he said almost angrily. "There was a five-minute span where I had to slip away to clear my head. I've wanted this for so long that it got kind of overwhelming. I hid on the other side of ReNEWed and tried to calm myself down. Unfortunately, it happened right in the middle of the time the police are asking about."

"Did you tell the chief where you were?" I asked him.

"Yes, and needless to say, it didn't go over very well. He kept asking me if anyone saw me. How would I know that?"

"Take it easy," I said, not wanting him to get overly excited. "Tell me about Simon."

Barton looked uncomfortable talking about the murder victim, but after a moment, he asked, "What do you want to know?"

"Were you two friends?" I asked.

"No, not really. We were rivals, competitors, and antagonists, but I don't think I would have called us friends," he admitted.

"Then why on earth was he here last night?"

"It's a fair question," Barton said. "He owed me big time, and I decided to cash in the debt. It was no secret that he wasn't happy being here, and the fact that he made a pass at Emma just made it that much worse. I was so angry I could have killed him."

I didn't think Barton even realized what he was saying, but talk like that would end him up in some very hot water indeed if the wrong people heard him saying it. "Never say that to anyone else ever again. Do you understand me?"

The chef nodded, looking shaken by my determination. Good. Maybe I was getting through to him. "Okay then. We're going on the assumption that you didn't have anything to do with the murder."

"Should I thank you for that?" Barton asked, half kidding.

"Probably, since it's more than the police are going to do," I said sternly. "We're also not going to focus our investigation on Emma, her mother, or her father. We know about Sherry West, Clint Harpold, and Shalimar Davis. Is there anything you can tell us about them?"

"Sherry has a nasty streak in her, and I always thought Simon was nuts for going out with her in the first place. Clint can be a good guy when he wants to be, but he's got a dark sense of humor, and there have been times that I've wondered if he might not legitimately be unbalanced, not that it's anything that would keep him from being a decent chef."

"What about Shalimar Davis?"

He looked uncomfortable when he heard the question. "What about her?"

"Barton, just exactly what kind of relationship do you have with her?"

"Now? There's no relationship at all. She owed me a favor. That's it," he said.

"How about before, though?" It suddenly dawned on me. "You didn't date her, did you?"

"We went out a few times," he admitted reluctantly. "Don't tell Emma, would you? I don't want her thinking badly of me."

"Listen, you've got a lot more problems than Emma right now," I said. "How did things end between you and Shalimar?"

"Badly," he said. "You've got to realize that this happened long before I met Emma."

"Exactly how long?" I asked, hoping for years.

"I broke it off with her a few weeks before I met Emma," he said.

It wasn't long enough, as far as I was concerned, but no one had murdered her, so we were safe, at least for now. "Okay. Is there anyone else we should speak with?"

"I'd talk to Clint. Nobody knows… knew Simon better than he did."

"Not even Sherry?"

"No. Take my advice. You can only trust half of what Sherry tells you, and with Shalimar, it's not even that much. Clint is probably somewhere around sixty-five, seventy percent."

"Fine, we'll keep that in mind. I don't need to tell you to keep a low profile, do I?"

Barton shrugged. "That's not going to be a problem. The hospital has asked me nicely to take a week's vacation until this blows over a bit. When I explained to them that I didn't have a week off to take, they told me it was their treat. How do you like that? It would be like someone telling you that you can't make donuts."

"I get it, but you really do need to stay out of trouble."

"Believe it or not, this is the first time anything like this has ever happened to me."

"I wish I could say the same thing," I said.

The kitchen door started to open, and before I could say another word, Barton took off like a shot.

"I thought I heard voices out here," Sharon said.

"I was talking to myself," I said. "That must have been what you heard."

She seemed to accept that explanation, which disturbed me a little, but at least I'd covered for Barton.

For now, anyway.

As the next few hours wore on, I fielded a dozen questions about the murder, but when my customers realized that I had no inside information and that I wasn't about to recount finding the body for them, they stopped asking fairly quickly.

It was a few minutes until ten when three very familiar faces showed up.

Had I honestly forgotten about another book club meeting? At least I'd read the book this time, though I'd detested it, so I was ready to discuss it with three of my favorite women in the world.

Jennifer, the leader of our little group, was a striking redhead, and she always dressed elegantly. She hugged me as she came in. "We just heard what happened last night. Are you okay?"

"I'm fine," I said, happy these women had stumbled into my life one day looking for a place to hold their meeting and embracing me as one of their own.

Hazel, a woman constantly on a diet but with a heart as big as could be, said, "Don't hog her, Jennifer. We want to hug her, too."

After she gave me a heartfelt embrace, Elizabeth said, "Now I feel peer pressure to hug you, too, whether I want to or not."

"That's okay, you don't have to," I said with a smile.

"I'm kidding," she said as she hugged me as well. Elizabeth loved to think of herself as a friend to authors everywhere. She was pen pals with several of the folks we'd read during our group discussions, and it was a matter of pride to her that there weren't many authors' addresses she couldn't track down one way or another. "Nobody gets my sense of humor."

"Not even your husband?" I asked her.

"Especially not him," Elizabeth said with a frown.

Oh, no. Had I just stepped into something inadvertently? "Is everything okay?"

"It's fine," she said, though clearly it wasn't.

It was just as obvious that she didn't want to talk about it, so I did my best to smile as I said, "This is my month to provide the treats, so help yourselves. It's on the house."

"Does that go for everybody?" Cal Jeffries asked. "If it is, I'll take a dozen bear claws to go, please."

"Cal, you have to be able to read to be in a book club," I said with a grin.

"Hey, I can read," he protested.

"I mean more than lottery numbers and stop signs," I replied. Cal loved to be kidded, and I did my best to tease him whenever I could.

The ladies didn't know that, though.

"Suzanne, is that any way to treat one of your customers?" Jennifer asked me.

Before I could explain, Cal did it for me. "Ma'am, I wouldn't come in here if Suzanne didn't zing me every now and then. It's more fun than the donuts."

"If you say so," she said, and then she quickly dismissed the conversation. "Let's see. I'll have a triple chocolate donut and a chocolate milk."

"That sounds good to me," Hazel added.

"I suppose you might as well make it three," Elizabeth chimed in, though it was clear her heart wasn't in it.

"That's a lot of chocolate, ladies," I said as I started gathering their orders.

Hazel looked at the tray I was making up. "Why are there four chocolate donuts and just as many glasses of chocolate milk, then?"

"Hey, I'm doing it, too. Besides, can you ever really have too much chocolate?"

"Not as far as I'm concerned," Hazel replied.

Once we were settled into our favorite area of the donut shop, Elizabeth pulled out the paperback in question that we'd been reading for this month's selection. She'd chosen it, so she got to lead the group discussion. "I know this book was a little dark, but I thought it was interesting. What did you all think about it?"

Hazel looked uncomfortable as she answered, "It was a little bit too graphic for me. The way Stella killed Angelo was... quite specific, wasn't it?"

We normally read cozy mysteries, so it had taken me some time to get into the book, however well written it might have been. That didn't mean I'd ever read the author again. Different tastes for different folks, but I liked my mysteries on the light side, and I wouldn't apologize for it to anyone. "I have to admit that I skipped that scene once she got out the electric carving knife." I shuddered again just thinking about it.

Jennifer did her best to put it in its best light. "I thought the descriptive nature of the narrative was extremely well done. I felt as though I was right there along with Stella as she hid from the police dogs. Wasn't that terrifying?"

"I could almost feel their breathing on the back of my neck," I offered.

Elizabeth suddenly put the book down on the table in front

of her. "Let's face it. I never should have chosen this book. Why did no one veto it last month when I brought it up?"

"We knew you were going through a rough patch," Jennifer said, patting Elizabeth's hand lightly. "Besides, a change every now and then couldn't hurt."

"That's clearly what my husband thinks," Elizabeth said with a frown.

"Now, Elizabeth, you don't know that for sure," Hazel said. "Remember when I suspected that *my* husband was cheating? It all turned out to be perfectly innocent in the end."

"Sure, but I *know* that's not the case for me."

I wanted to brighten the mood a little. "What did A.B. Yardling have to say when you contacted him?"

"He was short, dismissive, and entirely uninterested in having any kind of conversation with me," she said unhappily.

"Don't take it personally," I said, trying to make up for my misstep with her. "Most of the writers you get in touch with are absolutely delightful."

"Most are," she agreed. After taking a small bite of her donut, Elizabeth stood abruptly. "I'm sorry about today, but I really need to go."

Before anyone could stop her, Elizabeth raced out of the donut shop, with Jennifer close behind her.

Hazel paused long enough to explain, "Everything at home is falling apart for her. Bye. Thanks for the treats."

As I cleaned up after them, I couldn't help but feel bad for Elizabeth. I'd had enough troubles during my first marriage to Max to realize that life could be miserable in an unhappy relationship, and if there was anything I could do to help her, I'd do everything in my power to help my friend through it.

Unfortunately, at the moment, there was nothing I could do, so I decided to get back to work and see what else my day brought me.

CHAPTER 8

I WAS STILL FEELING A LITTLE blue about Elizabeth's situation when some of my favorite customers came in. Terri Milner, along with her twin daughters, Jerri and Mary, came into the shop bubbling over with excitement about something.

"Hey, Suzanne," Terri said, clearly worn out already, even though the day wasn't halfway over yet. "Load them up with whatever they want, would you?"

The girls were being themselves, rambunctious as ever. "Are you sure you want to give them a sugar fix?"

"We're going to the playground after we leave here, so they can run it all out of their systems. It's the only hope I have of getting a nap later."

"We're big girls," Jerri said proudly. "We don't take naps anymore."

"Naps are for sissies," Mary chimed in.

"Well then, Mommy is the biggest sissy in the world," Terri said. After the twins had modest treats and a pair of milks, Terri got a donut herself.

"When does school start back up?" I asked her.

"Eleven days, twenty-two hours and seven minutes," she said, barely glancing at her watch.

"Has it been a long summer?" I asked her, trying to suppress my grin.

"No, not really. I miss them terribly when they're gone, but

Harry's been traveling a lot for business this summer, and it's been a challenge taking care of them alone."

"Do they have any new crushes?" I asked, loving how openly adoring the girls were with their shared objects of affection. They both always liked the same boy, and it was never a problem for them, at least so far.

"Oh, yes. The flavor of the month is Mr. Garrison from the school."

"Isn't he a new teacher there?" I asked her.

"Yes, but I have to admit, the girls have good taste. Have you seen the man? He's absolutely divine."

"Does Harry have anything to worry about?" I asked her, still stinging a little from Elizabeth's problems.

"Not a chance. He's twenty-three years old, for goodness' sake. I don't have the energy for the two of them," she said with a grin as she pointed to her daughters. "No, my heart is safe with Harry." She said it with so much obvious love that it was exactly what I needed to counter my earlier experience with Elizabeth. I felt the same way about Jake that Terri did about her husband, and it was nice to see it in someone else.

"Mommy! There he is!" Both girls squealed and pointed out the window as the handsome young teacher walked by. He must have heard them through the window, because he gave them a big smile and a wave that sent them both diving into their seats for cover. He looked bemused by the situation, but once he was past, the girls raced toward their mother. "Come on. Let's go!"

Terri had no choice but to be swept up in their enthusiasm, and the three Milner women left the donut shop, stalking the teacher and clearly having a wonderful time doing it.

It was nearing eleven, and I knew that Grace would be along soon. Since we were out of customers at the moment and our stock was perilously low, I decided to shut the place down early. After I locked the door and flipped the sign, I carried the last bin of dirty dishes in back.

Sharon was finished working and sweeping an obviously already clean floor.

"We're shutting down early," I said. "Is that okay with you?"

"You're the boss," she said with a grin. "We close when you say we close. Let me get those."

After she emptied the bin's contents into the sink, I started working on the front, and before too long, we had the place ready for the next day.

"Do you think Emma might come back tomorrow?" I asked Sharon lightly.

She frowned at the question. "Why do you ask? Was there something I didn't do that I should have?" she asked, clearly a little put off by my question.

"You are a delight," I said. "I was just asking. The truth is, I missed her."

"If you don't mind, let's give her another day or two. She and I are set to run the shop in three days, and I'm sure she'll be up to it by then."

"If not, I don't have to take time off this week," I offered.

"Thanks, but I don't want her to have *too* much time on her hands, if you know what I mean. Suzanne, are you sure about that big tip?"

"I've never been more positive about anything in my life," I said with a grin.

"Okay. Thanks. I just wanted to make sure you were good with it."

"You can be," I said as I let her out. "Have a good afternoon, and I'll see you in the morning."

"I can't wait," she said, and then she was gone.

I was about to lock the door behind her when Grace rushed

up, wearing simple slacks and a nice blouse, which was quite a change from the suits she generally wore on the job. "Hey," she said nearly breathlessly.

"You didn't have to race over here. I'm not ready to go yet."

"No worries. I just wanted a donut before you threw them all out," she said.

"Take your pick," I said as I opened the three boxes of assorted leftovers.

"This looks great," she said, grabbing a honey donut I'd just added recently. I still wasn't sure about them myself, but enough folks liked them that they were staying on the menu, at least for the moment.

As I worked at finishing the deposit, my last task for the day at the donut shop, Grace sat there eating her donut and watching my every move.

"Wow, it appears that you get a snack *and* a show today," I said with a smile.

"I skipped breakfast," she explained. "Don't worry. I'll be able to eat lunch anytime. Are we going to the Boxcar?"

"Since we're going to Union Square anyway, I thought we might pop in and grab a bite at Napoli's, unless you have any objections," I said with a smile.

There weren't any, which I'd been suspecting would be the case. "That sounds great. After that, we can start digging around."

"Actually, I thought we might mix business and pleasure while we were there. I have a hunch that at least one of the DeAngelis girls knew Simon Reed, so I thought we might be able to get a little background on him and the folks he surrounded himself with."

"Will Angelica be okay with that?" Grace asked. We both knew that the matriarch of the clan loved us, but she was absolutely devoted to her girls.

"Don't worry, I'll get her permission before we start asking any questions," I assured her.

"Then hurry up and finish. I'm starving," she said, and then she popped the last bite of donut into her mouth.

"Poor neglected thing. You're just wasting away, aren't you?" I asked, smiling as I finished my deposit slip.

"Hey, you know I have a high metabolism," she protested.

"I do. It's one of the things I envy most about you. Well, that and your impeccable taste in best friends."

"I do have a solid track record there," she agreed.

Ten minutes later, the deposit finished and dropped off at the bank, we were in my Jeep and on our way to Union Square to see if we could track down Simon Reed's killer before things fell completely apart for my assistant, her family, and just about everybody she cared about in the world. I had a hunch that at least one of the DeAngelis girls would be able to help us in our search for background information, but even if they couldn't, we'd eat like royalty, and that was a win-win in my book if ever there was one.

"Suzanne! Grace! Welcome!" Angelica said as we walked into the kitchen at Napoli's. Not many folks had all-access passes like we did, but Grace and I had been of service to the DeAngelis women on more than one occasion in the past, so Angelica was always happy to see us.

"Hey, ladies," Sophia said as she frowned in concentration as she stared at a marble tabletop, which happened to be covered in rolled-out sheets of pasta.

"Trouble?" I asked her.

"No, I'm just trying to get the hang of this."

"Would you like some advice?" Angelica asked her youngest daughter.

"No thank you, Mother," she said grimly as she placed a scoop of what appeared to be a cheese blend on one section of the pasta.

"Suit yourself," Angelica said, and in a softer voice, she told us, "She's trying to develop a new type of ravioli. I don't think it's going to work, but why not let her experiment? What brings you two back into my kitchen? You're not just here to eat, are you?"

"What gave us away?" I asked her.

"If it was only food you were after, Maria would have seated you out front already," she said. Her daughter had tried to do just that, but we'd asked to be allowed into the kitchen, and Maria hadn't even had to consult with her mother.

"True enough. Did you hear what happened last night at Donut Hearts?" I asked her.

"We're not that far away, and besides, one of our own townsfolk was murdered. The entire area has been buzzing about it. I'm so sorry you had to find Simon's body, Suzanne."

"Did you know him well?" I asked gently. "If so, I'm sorry for your loss."

"Certainly it's a loss when *any* life is ended so short, but the young man certainly caused more than his fair share of trouble for me."

"Did it have anything to do with your restaurant?" I asked her.

"No, it was more to do with one of my daughters," she said.

"Sophia?" I asked softly.

"No, as a matter of fact, it was Maria," she said with a frown. "We all warned her not to get tangled up with that young man, but she wouldn't listen to us. Let's just say that it didn't end well."

"Was this recent?" I asked. The last thing I wanted was to

drag the DeAngelis clan into our murder investigation, but now that I knew one of the girls had dated the murder victim, I couldn't turn back.

"That depends. Do you consider eight months ago recent?" she asked me. "He told my Maria that he loved her, but then that redheaded tart came along, and suddenly he forgot all about my daughter."

"Let me get this straight," Grace said. "He dumped Maria for Sherry West? I can't even imagine how that is possible."

"Evidently Ms. West was quite a bit freer with her favors than my daughter was," Angelica said.

"Would you mind if we spoke with her about him?" I asked softly. "I don't want to stir up any bad memories for her, and if you refuse, we'll honor your request, but it might help us solve his murder."

"Are you investigating because you found the body, or because it happened in your shop?" Angelica asked me.

"Those two points are valid, but Emma asked us to look into it, and that's the driving reason. You see, Simon made a pass at her, a rather aggressive one, just before he was murdered. Not only is Emma under suspicion, but so are her mother and father, not to mention her boyfriend, Barton Gleason."

"The hospital chef," Angelica said with a nod. "He's quite good, isn't he?"

"You've eaten there yourself?" Grace asked her, clearly surprised by the idea.

"Why wouldn't I? When I heard all of the raves about his work, I sought him out. He's a delightful young man. He even invited me back into his kitchen." After a few moments of hesitation, Angelica nodded. "It's fine with me if you speak with Maria, but I have two conditions I must insist upon first."

"Name them," I said.

"You must respect Maria's wishes. If she doesn't want to talk to you about that dark period of her life, you both agree to drop your questioning immediately."

"I'm a little hurt that you would even feel as though you had to ask that," I said. "Angelica, I'd sooner cut off my own arm than trouble one of your children."

She patted my hand and smiled. "I know that, Suzanne, but when you and Grace investigate a case, sometimes your enthusiasm can be a little overwhelming."

I wanted to dispute the fact, but I couldn't. "Agreed. What's the second condition?"

"That you dine back here with us before you speak with her. She's too busy right now to talk anyway, so by the time you're finished eating, Sophia or I will take her place out front. Antonia is taking a well-deserved day off today, but we should be fine. What do you say?"

"Will you let us at least pay for our meal?" I asked her sternly.

"I will not," she said firmly.

"Half price?" I countered.

"No. On these two points I will not, I cannot budge."

"You heard the woman," Grace said as she tugged on my arm. "We wouldn't want to offend her." I glanced over and saw that she was grinning widely.

"Very well. You have a deal," I said, extending my hand.

Angelica shook it, and then she turned to Sophia. "How goes your experiment?"

"You're right," she said with a frown. "When I make them too big, they tend to fall apart in the water."

"Try reducing the portion by half," Angelica suggested. "It should be stable enough then."

"What's the use?" Sophia asked.

"Young lady, I did not raise you to be a quitter. If this is a success, I'll even let you name the dish when we offer it on the menu."

"Could I call it Loads of Yummy Goodness?" Sophia asked.

"You may not!" Angelica protested, at least until she saw her daughter's broad grin. "You, young lady, will be the death of me someday."

Sophia hugged her mother as she said, "I certainly hope it's not anytime soon."

"Why are you both still standing?" Angelica asked as she turned to look at us. "Take a seat. Your food will be ready soon."

"But we didn't even order yet," Grace protested.

"Please. As my guests, I will choose your meals, unless you insist otherwise."

I didn't need to see Sophia shaking her head from side to side to know how to respond to that. "I'm sure that whatever you serve us will be wonderful."

"Very well," Angelica said, and then she turned to her daughter. "Let's give them the new sampler you've been working on."

Sophia frowned for a moment. "Are you sure? That's a lot of food, Mom."

Angelica shrugged. "Make it a smaller size then, but offer all of the same dishes," she said. "Lunch for two."

"We should offer *that* as a special," Sophia said lightly. "We could serve it on Tuesdays and call it Two For Tuesday."

"I like that," Angelica said, clapping her hands together.

"I was just kidding," Sophia protested.

"Well, I am not. One Two For Tuesday special, coming right up."

"But it's not even Tuesday," Sophia said, putting up her last bit of resistance.

"It's close enough," Angelica said.

Soon enough, Grace and I were presented with a platter between us, with enough food for at least four people from the looks of it. There were offerings of lasagna, ravioli, spaghetti with meatballs, and a hearty salad making up the fourth quadrant.

"Dig in," Angelica said as she served us with a flourish.

"Are you sure there should be this much food for two people?" Grace asked as she surveyed the offering.

"No worries, my friends. If there's any left, I'll box it up for you," Angelica said.

I grinned at Grace and began to fill my plate. She did the same, and as we ate, we had a pleasant chat with Angelica and Sophia. No one mentioned Simon Reed, and it was a pleasant interlude as bite after bite exploded with delicious flavor in my mouth. The pasta, homemade every day, was like nothing I'd ever had anywhere else, and the meatball was large enough to nearly dominate that portion of my plate. "What's in this?" I asked as I took another bite.

"It's a blend of three meats and six spices," Angelica explained.

"Don't ask her the spice mix ingredients," Sophia said with a grin. "Even we don't know all of her recipes and mixes."

"In good time, my love. In good time I will share them with you all."

"I'm just saying, I'd hate for them to be lost to the ages if something sudden should happen to you," Sophia said. "Not only would we all be grief stricken, but Napoli's couldn't continue without the Angelica DeAngelis special touch."

I looked to see if the youngest daughter was smiling, but she was deadly serious. Angelica studied her child for a moment before replying. "Thank you for that sentiment, Sophia, but if that should happen, you and your sisters will find everything written down in a small journal safely housed at the bank."

"Which bank?" Sophia asked, smiling to break the somber tone that had just arisen.

"That you will have to discover for yourselves," Angelica said with a laugh. "Think of it as one last treasure hunt."

"I hope it's a hundred years before we have to search for it," she said, hugging her mother as she said it.

"Well, perhaps not a hundred. Let's say fifty, shall we?"

"I'm not sure I'll be ready to let you go so soon," Sophia said.

"That was amazing," I said as I pushed my plate back. To my surprise, Grace and I had managed to polish off nearly every bite on the platter.

"You see?" Angelica asked with a smile as she put her arms on both our shoulders. "I knew you could do it. Now, who is ready for dessert?"

"There is no way I can eat another bite," I said. "Grace?"

"I should have stopped ten minutes ago, but my gluttony got the best of me," she answered.

"Then I'll send some home with you," Angelica said.

"Please don't. We'll be spending the afternoon in Union Square, and I'd hate for it to spoil." I was about to offer to pay something, at least a token, to make up for all we'd eaten, but Angelica must have read my mind. She gave me a look that expressed her displeasure with the very thought of what I was about to suggest, so I changed course abruptly. "Thank you for the meal. It was amazing."

"You are most welcome," she said as she nodded and added a smile as well. Angelica turned to Sophia and asked, "Would you mind relieving your sister and asking her to join us in the kitchen?"

"Aw, man, I hate waiting on customers," Sophia said.

"Yes, but here we rotate jobs. Even I work the front occasionally."

"Not as often as I do," Sophia mumbled.

"What was that?"

"I said that's what I do," she answered with a grin as she winked at me.

Angelica chuckled, and then Sophia was gone.

"Remember our agreement," Angelica told us once we were alone.

"We promise," I said.

"Absolutely," Grace replied.

"Very good. I know I can trust you girls."

"But you're staying anyway, right?" I asked her with a smile.

"Can you honestly say that you are surprised?" Angelica asked, matching my grin with one of her own.

"The only thing that would have surprised me would have been if you'd taken the front and let Sophia stay," I said.

Maria came back, frowning. "What's this I hear from Sophia? You don't really want to talk to me about that rat, Simon Reed, do you?"

Well, things were certainly getting off to a rocky start.

CHAPTER 9

"**M**OM, DO I REALLY HAVE to talk about this?" Maria asked her mother. "I'm starving."

"You may do as you please, but I'd be most appreciative if you would help Suzanne and Grace in any way that you can. Need I recount all of the times they've stepped up to help us in the past?"

"Hang on, Angelica. That's not the way this is going to work," I said. "Maria, you don't have to say anything to us if you don't want to. Your mother agreed to let us ask you some questions, but you're certainly under no obligation to answer any of them."

Maria looked from me to Grace to her mother, who nodded once. "It's true. Whether you answer or not is your decision."

"But you'd like me to, wouldn't you?" Maria asked.

"You always were a bright child," Angelica said with a smile as she plated some food for her daughter. All of the DeAngelis women were lovely, but none more so than the matriarch of the clan. Still, the very thought that a young man would willingly break up with Maria, whose inner beauty outshone even her outer appearance, was beyond me. Simon Reed was evidently many things, including a fool, when it came to matters of the heart.

As Maria started to eat, she said, "Go on. Fire away. Soph hates being out front, so I promised her I wouldn't take too long to eat."

"Your sister will find a way to survive the ordeal," Angelica said bluntly.

"Sure. Okay." As Maria took another bite, she looked at us expectantly.

"First things first," I said. "Who do you know who might want to kill Simon?"

"Do you mean besides me?" she asked, and then she saw her mother's instant disapproval and quickly amended, "Strike that. Simon had a polarizing effect on people. You either loved him or hated him. Let me tell you, when I was with him, he made me feel as though I was the only person in the universe that mattered. He hung on every word I said, and he actually listened! Do you know how rare that is to find in guys my age?"

"Men of any age, I'd say," Angelica said glumly. She hadn't had much luck dating in recent years, and I had to wonder if it wasn't because she was such an intimidating package.

"So, he was smooth," Grace said.

"It goes beyond that," Maria explained between bites. "I honestly thought we were in love, but the moment Sherry West set her sights on him, I was sunk. That girl would do anything in her power to get what she wanted, and woe to anyone who might get in her way."

"Did she threaten you?" I asked.

"Not in so many words, but she made it clear that if I crossed her, I'd pay for it. I have a feeling Simon finally met his match with that one."

"Do you think she'd be capable of violence?" I asked Maria.

"Oh, yes. She loves living up to the fiery redhead image."

"Who else might be angry enough to kill him?" I asked.

"Have you met Shalimar yet?" Maria asked with a shake of her head. "She dated him before I came along, and from what I've heard, she kept trying to get Simon back, even when we were together."

"She's on our list, but we haven't spoken with her yet. Do you have any idea where we might find her?" I asked.

"She's working over at the Lazy Eye café," Maria said.

"I've never heard of it, and I thought I knew everything about Union Square," I said.

"It's brand new. Simon's roommate, Clint Harpold, just opened the place last week."

"We'll definitely head there first then," I said. "How did Clint and Simon get along?" Since we'd heard conflicting stories about the pair, I wanted to see what Maria had to say.

"Not great, but to be fair, not many men got along with Simon," she said. "I don't know if they were better or worse than most, though."

"Is there anyone else you can think of?" I asked.

"Have you talked to Simon's brother yet?" Maria asked after she finished another hearty bite. How did this girl manage to eat so much and stay so slim? If she was giving lessons, I wanted to be the first one to sign up for the course.

"We didn't even know that he had a brother," Grace admitted.

"Oh, yes. Theo is a real treat."

"Theo?" I asked.

"Short for Theodore. He works at an investment firm downtown, and he absolutely hated his brother."

"Why?" I asked, curious about how some sibling rivalries were so intense.

"When their dad died, Simon inherited one bank account and Theo got another. Why they didn't split things equally among themselves was beyond me, but Simon ended up getting five thousand dollars more than Theo. We were dating at the time, and Theo told Simon that he had nine months to make things right, or he was going to do something about it himself."

"When would the nine months expire?" Grace asked.

"Probably right about now," Maria admitted. "Do you think he actually might have done it?"

"That's what we're trying to find out. Is there anything else you might be able to tell us, Maria?"

She finished the last of the food on her plate as she shook her head. "No, sorry. The truth is that I've done my best to get him out of my mind. It still makes me sad that someone killed him. Nobody deserves to die that way, especially so young. I don't know. If he'd been given more time, maybe Simon would have found a way to turn things around."

"Maybe," I said, highly doubting that this particular leopard would have ever been able to change his spots. "Thanks for taking the time to talk to us about something that was obviously so painful for you."

"It's fine," Maria said. Before she made her way back out front, she kissed her mother's cheek. "You were right. I'm glad I talked to them."

"I'm very proud of you," Angelica said.

"You know what? I'm proud of me, too."

After she was gone, I said, "Angelica, I may not have told you this recently, but you've raised a fine crop of young ladies."

"I know, but I always enjoy hearing it," she said. "Now, if there's nothing else we can do for you, I must get back to work."

"You've done more than enough." I surprised us both by hugging her before we left, and Grace joined in as well. Angelica looked flustered for a moment, but it took her only an instant to return our embrace in full.

"Good luck," she said as we headed for the back door in order to avoid going out through the front.

"Thanks. At this point, we need all that we can get," I said.

"Why would anyone call their restaurant the Lazy Eye?" Grace asked me as we followed the directions Maria had given us.

"It's odd and quirky, anyway. Who knows? Maybe there's a story behind it," I said. "Then again, maybe it's due to a complete lack of creativity on Clint Harpold's part."

"Why do you say that?" Grace asked.

"Look at the sign," I said. Perched above the new café, at least new under this ownership, was the word DINER spelled out in big red letters. There was just one problem with it, though. The "I" had slipped down a good ten inches and dangled precariously above the door. "Get it? It's a lazy 'I.'"

"Why didn't they just fix the letter and come up with a new name?" Grace asked me.

"Feel free to ask Clint Harpold that after we finish up with our questions about Simon Reed," I said.

"I'll pass," she said as we parked and got out.

The place was fairly empty, given the time of day. Napoli's had been busy when we'd walked through the front door coming in, but then again, some time had passed since, and we had exited through the rear of the building. Still, the parking lot had been full there, whereas here there was enough room to park a dump truck and still have space left over.

As we walked in, a brassy blonde wearing a tight T-shirt and a short denim skirt handed us a pair of menus before we could say a word. Her hair was like a mane, full and flowing, with streaks of green, pink, blue, and red throughout. I could see what the chief meant. She certainly looked memorable! Her name tag, barely holding on to the thin material, said that her name was Shalimar. Surely there couldn't be two of them. "Welcome to the Lazy Eye," she said in a bored manner. "Would you like to hear the lunch specials?"

"Thanks, but we already ate," I said as I looked around. It had clearly been a diner for a long time. There were signs of neglect from years of abuse from the scuffed floors to the cracking vinyl on the booths.

"Then it's a good thing you came to a restaurant, isn't it?" she asked sarcastically. "If you don't order something, you can't stay."

I was about to tell her why we were really there, to talk to her and her boss about the late Simon Reed, when Grace surprised me by asking, "We've had our lunch, but we're not quite full. What's on the dessert menu?"

Could she really eat another bite? I wasn't sure that I could manage it. I'd just felt more and more full since we'd left Napoli's, and I wasn't at all certain I could force down a single bite, no matter how good it might be.

"The cherry pie is excellent," she said as we took seats at the counter up front. It put us close to her, and the kitchen as well.

"Excellent. We'll split a piece," I said.

When Shalimar frowned, Grace added, "Go ahead and make that two. I'm feeling a bit hungry after that lunch."

She was obviously lying now, but I wasn't going to challenge her on it. "Two it is," I said as I held up two fingers.

Shalimar opened the Plexiglas carousel and removed two slices of cherry pie. As she put one down in front of me, I marveled at the flaky golden crust, the abundant cherries and filling that spilled out on either side, as well as the generous nature of the portion. If it tasted anything as good as it looked, I might just have to force myself to sample it.

"Are these freshly baked?" I asked her.

"The boss makes them every day," she said as she slid one bill between us. We hadn't even gotten our first bites in, and she was already looking to get paid.

I tried a small bite and was rewarded with a burst of goodness in my mouth. I wasn't sure what else Clint Harpold might be, but he could bake a pie, there was no doubt about that. "Wow," I said.

Grace tried hers as well, with similar results. "Is the baker around? I'd love to compliment her," she said, purposefully missing Clint's gender.

"She happens to be a 'he,'" Shalimar said. "Hang on a second." She walked to the window and said, "Clint. Two women want to compliment you on your pie."

"I asked you to call me Chef, Shalimar," he scolded her as he came out of the kitchen wearing a white smock with long sleeves and a hat, despite the heat and the lack of a fully functioning air conditioner in the diner. In my opinion, he was a tad overdressed for being in a diner, but then again, he could wear a clown outfit for all I cared if he kept making pie that good. He turned to us and did his best to smile. "I'm the chef here."

"This pie is wonderful," I said. "How do you do it?"

"I can't give away my secrets, but I appreciate the praise."

Grace looked at him oddly for a moment before she spoke. "Did our waitress just call you Clint?"

He looked embarrassed. "Yes. What can I say? Good help is hard to find." He'd said it fairly low, but evidently Shalimar had picked up on it.

"I know when I'm not wanted. I'm going on break," she said with a frown.

"But you just took one," Clint protested.

"I didn't know we were keeping score," she said as she walked out without another word.

"You aren't Clint *Harpold*, are you?" Grace asked him.

"Yes, I am. Why? Have you heard of me?" He was clearly flattered by having his name recognized, but I had a hunch that he wasn't going to like it for long.

Grace didn't disappoint me. "You were Simon Reed's roommate, weren't you? I can't believe you came into work today after he was murdered last night."

"It's a real shame, but I can't afford to shut the diner down for anything short of a hurricane."

"Were you two very close?" I asked him.

"We went to school together," Clint said dismissively.

I pretended to recognize him all of a sudden. "I thought you looked familiar. You were working at Barton Gleason's pop-up bistro in April Springs last night, weren't you?"

He looked unhappy about being tied with the endeavor at all. "I was there to return a favor."

"So, when was the last time you saw Simon alive?" Grace asked.

"I have no idea. Things were crazy in the outdoor kitchen. The truth is I didn't even realize that Simon was gone until somebody screamed something about murder."

I resented the implication that I'd screamed, but maybe he was talking about someone else. "Who would do such a thing?" I asked.

"You mean besides the obvious answer, which was everyone who ever knew him?" Clint asked, showing his true feelings at last.

"Was he really that bad?" I asked.

"The man had the morals of an alley cat," he said with a shrug. "I'm sure some people will try to gloss his actions over now that he's gone, but I'm not one of them. You wouldn't believe the stories I could tell you about some of his little adventures, as he liked to call them."

I took a bite of pie, smiled appropriately, and then I said, "We love dirt! What do you have that's juicy?" Then I turned to Grace and said, "We have to tell Sylvia about this place. She'll want him to cater the next formal ball once we tell her how good the food is here. How many people attended last year?"

"I believe it was two hundred and fifty," Grace said. Even for a fictional number, I thought it was much too high and entirely impossible to believe, but evidently Clint didn't have that problem. "Plus, you know how Syl loves gossip. If we can give her a story about the chef's roommate, it will be a cinch that she'll book him just to hear his best escapades."

That was all it took to open Clint up. He leaned on the counter and said softly, "Ladies, you wouldn't believe what that scoundrel was up to. Not only was he dating one of the waitresses working last night, but he made a pass at another one! Then, to top things off, a jealous husband came by looking for him! I sent the man off on a wild goose chase, or Simon was going to be in big trouble." Clint frowned at the thought as he added, "Maybe I should tell the police about David Clifton and his wife, Rosa, now that I think about it."

"Ooh, that sounds juicy enough," I said. "Was she there as well?"

He shrugged again. "I thought I caught a glimpse of her just before her husband showed up. She was Simon's boss, did you know that?"

"Does she own a restaurant as well?" Grace asked. "My, I never knew Union Square had so many good places to eat."

"No, Simon spent his days selling office supplies at Clifton's over on Second," he said. "He couldn't get a real job as a chef."

"Like you and Barton did, right?" Grace asked.

Clint looked at her suspiciously. "How exactly do you know Barton?"

I came up with an answer to that before Clint got too suspicious. "We've eaten at the hospital cafeteria. He's really quite good, isn't he?"

"If you care for that sort of food," Clint said dismissively. I had to fight the impulse to defend Barton's food, since that wasn't why we were there.

"Do you have any other tidbits we might share with good old Sylvia?" I asked.

Clint was about to answer when a pair of businessmen walked in and looked around. "Are you open for lunch?"

"Yes, sir," he said as he grabbed two menus and hustled toward them. I saw that Shalimar was still outside taking her extended break, even though the men had been forced to walk around her to get inside. I wasn't sure how desperate Clint was for waitstaff, but he had to be able to do better than that. I took another bite of pie despite how full I was, and then I slapped a five on the counter. It would cover the bill, though just barely, but I didn't feel too bad about it. Shalimar's service had been less than acceptable, and while I believed in tipping generously when someone made a real effort, I was also notorious for cutting one to the bone when it proved otherwise.

"Thanks," I said as we rushed out the door.

"Would you like a business card for your friend?" Clint asked, desperately patting his pockets and finally producing one.

I took it and slid it into my jeans. "Thanks again. The money's on the counter. Sorry to eat and run, Chef, but we really have to dash."

"We're meeting Bunny at the Country Club," Grace said lightly. "And you don't keep Bunny waiting long."

And before the chef could protest, we were out the door.

CHAPTER 10

SHALIMAR IGNORED US AS WE were leaving, so I walked within six inches of her and stopped dead in my tracks.

"Can I help you with something in particular?" she asked in a surly manner.

"You were so nice to us inside, we wanted to stop by and say thank you personally," I said, lying through my teeth. "Your boss was telling us about his roommate."

"Yeah, well, Clint talks too much."

"Were you an admirer of Simon's cooking?" I asked her.

"Lady, I was a lot more than that until that Italian tramp came along and stole him away from me."

I really had to bite my tongue. Calling Maria DeAngelis a tramp was outrageous, and I was about to comment despite knowing better when Grace grabbed my arm.

"You two really dated?" she asked the waitress.

"We were destined to be together," Shalimar said. "Only Simon wasn't ready to accept it yet."

"I thought he was seeing a cute little redhead," I said, doing my best to goad her into saying something she might regret.

"Cute? That barracuda? Simon was getting ready to dump her. We were going to get together again as soon as he made it happen. At least that's what he promised me two nights ago."

"But we heard he made a pass at another girl just last night," I said.

"Boy, good old Clint sure does like to talk, doesn't he?" she asked.

"It is true, though, isn't it?"

"That's what most people didn't get. Simon was just friendly by nature. If somebody took his outgoing personality the wrong way, that was their problem, not his. I'm sure he didn't mean anything by it. Like I said, we were going to get back together."

It sounded as though she was doing her best to convince herself, not us. "Didn't it make you mad though, given the way he treated women?" I asked her.

She tensed up so much that I was afraid the waitress was going to come after me for one second, but she managed to bite back her temper at the last second. "He treated me just fine. Besides, I don't see how that's any of your business."

"You're the one who brought it up," Grace said, goading her as well. I wasn't sure it was the best plan of action anymore, but we didn't get a chance to find out.

The front door of the diner opened, and Clint popped his head out, clearly upset about his waitress's continued absence. "If you want to work here, then work, Shalimar."

"Keep your shorts on. I'm coming," she said, giving us both wicked stares as she returned.

"I hope to hear from you soon, ladies," Clint said, trying to salvage his little outburst with a clearly insincere smile.

"Oh, you will, but for now, we really do need to go. Bunny won't wait forever," Grace said, and we got into my Jeep and drove off.

"Bunny?" I asked once we were away from the restaurant, trying to fight a smile.

"I was going to say Buffy, but I couldn't bring myself to do it. Wow, Simon was not afraid of taking his swings at the plate when it came to women, was he?"

"I have a hunch that he batted one too many times," I said. "Can you believe that he was having an affair with a married woman while dating Sherry West, *and* he still found time to make a pass at Emma? When did he find the time to cook?"

"I don't have any idea," Grace said. "I take it we're going to the office supply store now to speak with Mr. and Mrs. Clifton."

"We could do that, or we could always go talk to Theodore Reed. It's your call, but we need to talk to all three of them this afternoon."

"Let's talk to Theo first," Grace said. "After that, we might have to divide and conquer the married couple. You know, I never understood why anyone would have an affair. If you aren't happy with your partner, just leave them and start fresh with someone else." I must have given something away by my chilly expression, because Grace quickly added, "Suzanne, I'm so sorry. I didn't mean anything by it. I wasn't talking about you."

"It's okay," I said. "I wanted to ask Max the same question, but I never managed to get around to it. I was just too angry with him, I guess. Trust me, if I'd known he was fooling around with Darlene, I would have ended it immediately. In a way, I suppose that I did. The second I caught them together, I started divorce proceedings."

"I didn't mean to bring up the past," she said, apologizing again.

I patted her hand and did my best to smile. "My past brought me to where I am today, and that's with the man I love. I can't ask for more than that."

"How's Jake doing, by the way?"

"He's got problems of his own," I said, not really wanting to get into the drama with Paul at the moment. "How should we tackle Theodore? Should we approach him as inquiring amateur sleuths, or would you like to invent a cover story to spice it up a little?"

Grace lit up at the suggestion. "Let's come up with something fun. I can be a bank examiner and you can be a federal agent."

"That's a little complicated, don't you think?"

"Maybe," she said with a frown. "I know. We can be reporters again. I *love* when we do that."

"I'm okay with that," I said. We'd used the ruse in past investigations, and I knew how much Grace liked pretending to be other people. "Do you think he'll talk to us if he thinks we're writing a story about his brother?"

"Maybe not," she said, vetoing the idea just as I was getting myself in character. "We could always say that we owe Simon money. From what we've heard, Theodore seems to be driven that way."

"I don't know about you, but my wallet's pretty bare at the moment." That was true of just about every moment, so now wasn't all that much out of the ordinary.

"We don't have to say how *much* we owe him," Grace said. "Would twenty do it?"

"If Theodore answers our questions, I'd be willing to chip in ten myself."

"No, this one's on me. Consider it my treat, and I won't take no for an answer."

"Then I won't object," I said with a grin.

"It appears that his office is in a strip mall," I said as I pulled into the place Grace directed me to park. She'd used her phone to look up the address and then a mapping program to lead us there. I had to say, the office was less than impressive.

"These things spawn overnight, don't they?" Grace asked me.

"Not only that, but the businesses seem to change from

month to month. I wonder what the investment firm office will be in six months?"

"My guess is it will either be a chiropractor's office or a frozen yogurt place," she said. "Care to make a wager?"

"Maybe we're selling Theodore Reed short. He might be really good at what he does."

"Maybe, but would he still be here if he were?" she asked me.

"That's a good point," I said. "Let's go have ourselves a chat with Simon's brother."

"I'm right behind you. Should I take the lead, or would you like to?"

I usually liked leading the questioning in our investigations, but I also realized that Grace loved playing a role herself. She'd missed her calling, but I was glad she wasn't a professional con artist. "You can do it."

"Oh goody," she said as she rubbed her hands together. "This is going to be fun."

"Don't forget why we're doing this," I reminded her gently.

"There's nothing that says we can't have a little fun too, is there?"

"Not that I know of," I admitted.

"Then let's go."

Theo Reed had tried to make his office look impressive, outfitting it with quartersawn oak furniture and fancy accessories, but ultimately it was still a small rental space in a strip mall, something he couldn't easily disguise. The man himself was balding prematurely, and he'd developed a bit of a potbelly that he tried unsuccessfully to conceal with a three-piece suit. Looking up from his desk, he said, "Welcome, ladies. I'm sorry. Did you have an appointment?"

"No. We thought we'd just pop in on you," Grace said.

Before she could get into her story, he shuffled some paperwork on his desk and frowned. "I have a tight schedule, but I may be able to carve out a few minutes for you."

His plans for the day probably included doing the crossword puzzle, but I thought it was impolite to point that out. "Thanks so much," I said.

"No worries. Now, how much are you thinking about investing? I must tell you that the market is hot right now, but I'm not sure how long it's going to hold on, so the sooner we can get started on building your portfolios, the more you'll make in the long run."

"You sound so certain," I said, getting off track from our original intent. It was just that he sounded so confident about something that I knew could be quite volatile. "How can you be so sure?"

"I've been doing this a very long time," he said, "and I've trained with some of the brightest investment minds in the country."

I looked around but couldn't see a single diploma. "Who exactly have you studied with?"

"Does the name Barrington Kraft ring a bell?" he asked.

"Do you actually know him?" Grace asked, clearly as skeptical as I was that this man ever worked with one of the best investors alive.

"No, not personally, but I have worked with one of his former employees, which is just as good as sitting at the feet of the master himself," he said.

For all we knew, Kraft's former employee could have been his gardener, but we were heading in the wrong direction.

"We're getting off track. You see, we're not here to invest," I said.

Grace looked at me oddly, and I realized that I had just done to her what she often did to me. I'd stepped in when she was in charge. She didn't seem too pleased being on the other end of it, and I could clearly relate to the feeling.

"We need to discuss your brother with you," Grace said.

Theodore shut down as quickly as if a switch had just been thrown. "I have no desire to discuss that situation with anyone. You're not reporters, are you? I absolutely detest reporters."

So, we'd made a good decision to abandon that particular cover for our questions. Grace said, "No. As a matter of fact, we've got some money that belongs to Simon. We don't know who to pay it back to, and we were hoping you could help us."

Theodore's mood lightened considerably. "I'll be glad to relieve you of that burden."

"Are you the estate's executor?" Grace asked him.

"I'm his closest living relative," the investment broker said. "I can assure you that I'll make sure the money goes to the proper parties involved."

Probably meaning his own pocket, unless I missed my guess. "I thought you two were estranged," I said, once again stepping on Grace's toes. I didn't seem to be able to help myself. I'd have to be easier on Grace the next time our roles were reversed. It was truly difficult to sit there quietly and watch the investigation unfold in someone else's hands.

"Where did you hear that?" he asked sharply.

"It's common knowledge, Theo," Grace said.

"Actually, I prefer Theodore," he corrected her primly.

"Theodore it is," Grace said, never skipping a beat. "There was a money issue between you, correct?"

"That was a long time ago. We put that behind us."

"When was the last time you saw him?" Grace asked.

"Sometime last week, I suppose," he said rather vaguely. "Now, about that money. How much exactly are we talking about?"

Grace frowned. "I'm still not sure we should just hand it

over to you. Honestly, we didn't expect to find you working today. Aren't you handling your brother's arrangements?"

"I had to come into the office for a few important meetings with clients," he said dismissively. "I'll be seeing to all of that later." He glanced at his watch, clearly a knockoff Rolex, and then he added, "I really must insist that we move this along. As you said yourself, I have a great many things to see to today."

His brusque nature was bothering me. Couldn't the man garner at least a little bit of sympathy for his dead brother? It was very clear we weren't getting anything else out of him. "We'll need a receipt, of course," I said.

Grace looked at me oddly, and it took me a moment to realize that she was trying to keep from smiling.

"Of course," he said. "Will you be writing a check, or paying cash?"

"Oh, it's cash," she said as she pulled out a five from her wallet.

"Seriously? You want a receipt for five dollars? Are you certain that's all you owed my late brother?"

"Actually, it was four dollars and seventy-five cents," Grace said with a smile. "You don't happen to have change, do you?"

It was all I could do to keep from laughing as Theodore said, "Sorry."

"Fine. Keep it," Grace said as she started to stand.

I stayed put, though.

"Was there something else I could do for you?" he asked me, clearly irritated with both of us that we'd wasted his time.

"The receipt you promised would be nice," I said, doing my best to look as though I had nowhere else in the world I needed to be.

In an angry hand, he jotted something down on a sheet of legal paper and thrust it across his desk at us. "Thanks for stopping by."

I carefully picked up the receipt by one edge. "Thank you. Have a nice day. Again, we are sorry for your loss."

"Okay," he said.

Once we were outside, Grace started laughing. "I thought he was going to pop a blood vessel when you asked him for a receipt. Nice job jabbing him a little."

"I didn't do it out of spite," I said as I carefully tried to fold the letter with a minimal amount of touching. "I thought his fingerprints might come in handy."

"I thought Stephen said that he'd identified all of the prints in your kitchen."

"He did, but what could it hurt having these as well?" I asked as I tucked the folded paper into my back pocket. "Sorry about the way I acted in there."

"How's that?"

"I kind of got a little carried away," I admitted. "You were supposed to be running the questioning, but I kept talking."

"It's okay. It's hard to keep quiet, isn't it?" she asked me with a grin.

"Apparently," I admitted. "I hope we have better luck with the Cliftons."

"We couldn't have much worse, could we?"

"Oh, I don't know. Never say never. I know you aren't going to like it, but I say we tackle them head on with the truth this time."

"Why not?" Grace asked. "Which truth do you think we should use?"

"That we've heard she was having an affair with Simon and that she was spotted near the scene of the crime last night," I said.

"Wow, the direct approach. I like it," Grace said.

"Then we have a plan."

CHAPTER 11

THE OFFICE SUPPLY STORE WAS small by most standards, and I wondered how they managed to stay in business. Their competitors, probably big-box stores and Internet giants, surely beat them on pricing, selection, and availability. Shops like it were dying everywhere across the country, and I wondered when and not if our shopping culture would change forever. At least no one had been able to figure out a way to sell and ship fresh donuts online yet, but there was no doubt in my mind that sometime in the future, it would probably happen, though I doubted it would be in my lifetime.

A pretty brunette in her early thirties was sitting behind a desk going through stacks of paperwork. She was alone, which was what I'd been hoping for, and what was more, she appeared to have been crying, and recently, too.

"May I help you?" she asked.

"That depends. Are you Rosa Clifton?" I asked her.

"I am," she said brightly, doing her best to sound cheerful. "Did someone recommend me to you? I can offer you competitive prices and fast shipping as well as personal service for whatever your office supply needs are."

It was a pitch I was sure she gave to every new customer that walked through the door, but we weren't even pretending to be buyers at the moment. "We're here about Simon Reed."

That shut down her smile instantly. "It was a real tragedy, losing him like that," she said automatically.

"Professionally or personally?" Grace asked her.

"Pardon me? Simon was a part-time employee here. Of course he'll be missed, but there was nothing personal about our relationship."

"Funny, that's not what we heard," Grace said softly.

"I don't have the time or the energy for people who have nothing better to do than spread lies and rumors."

"We spoke with someone who should know, Rosa. You were also spotted at the pop-up bistro last night right around the time of the murder. Have the police been here yet to speak with you?" I asked her.

"Or do they even know about your relationship with Simon yet?" Grace asked. She then looked at me as she added, "Maybe we should tell them."

"Please. Don't," she said, grabbing our arms simultaneously. "My husband can't find out."

"We heard that he already knows," I said. I wanted to be sympathetic to this woman's plight, but she'd had an affair with the murder victim while being married to someone else, and that particular sin was a tough one for me to swallow, since I'd experienced it from the other side myself. "In fact, he was there, too."

"I thought he was there for the food after Simon told us both about the bistro," she said weakly. "And then I realized that he had no interest in the cuisine. He was following me, waiting to catch us together! You've got to help me. I'm afraid for my life!"

"If you need help, you should call the police," Grace said.

"That's what we're going to do," I added.

"Please don't!" she pled with us.

"Rosa, they need to know," I said as a big, heavyset man came out of the back room.

"I thought I heard voices out here," he said good-naturedly. "Ladies, welcome to our store."

Rosa begged us with her gaze not to say anything about Simon. I understood her need for us to cooperate, but we were investigating the man's death. How could we not talk about him? "We were good friends with one of Simon Reed's friends," I said.

"Yeah, that was a real shame what happened to him," David said with a frown. "Do they have any idea who did it yet?"

Was that a casual question, or did he have a more personal reason for asking? "From what we've heard, the police are still tracking down suspects. Were you at the restaurant where he was attacked last night?"

David Clifton shrugged. "Sure, I decided to swing by at the last minute. Simon said the guy cooking there was pretty good, so I popped in for a bite. I didn't want to wait for a table though, so I took off before the fireworks started." So, he'd just admitted being at the crime scene, but he was trying to divert our suspicion away from himself at the same time.

"Did anyone happen to see you leave?" Grace asked him.

"Probably, but nobody I could name," he answered with a shrug. "You were there, Rosa. Did you happen to see me leave?"

"I didn't see you there," she said in a meek voice.

"Are you sure about that?" he asked as he took a step toward her. "I could swear that I saw you there, too."

"Maybe I did see you after all," she said in a voice so soft I barely heard it. "I'm not sure."

Her husband seemed to stare at her quizzically for a full minute, though I knew that it was probably just a few seconds. Then he shook his head as he stepped away from her and turned to us. "Sorry. We can't help you. Did you happen to need any office supplies today?"

"No, that's not why we're here," Grace said.

"Well, that's the entire reason that we are, so if you'll excuse us, we have work to do." The dismissal was clear, and I didn't want to push him on it just yet.

"Thanks for your time," I said, and Grace and I left.

"Should we call the police and report him?" Grace asked the moment we were outside.

"For what, exactly? He might be gruff, but I'm not sure he can be arrested for his attitude."

"Did you not see how scared Rosa was of him?" Grace asked. "Suzanne, I know infidelity is a hot button for you, but we can't just leave without doing something."

"What do you propose we do?" I asked her. "I'm serious, Grace. If she wants out of her marriage, she's going to have to find a way to do it herself. If I could help her, I would. I just don't know where to start."

"I'm calling Stephen," she said as she reached for her phone.

"This isn't even in his jurisdiction," I reminded her.

"Maybe not, but he'll know what to do." The call went straight to his voicemail though, so after leaving him a brief message, she put her phone away and turned to me. "Is it just me, or did we make things worse than they were when we got here?"

"It feels that way, doesn't it? Let's go back in and see if we can get her out of there," I said.

"Why the sudden change of heart?" she asked me.

"It's not all that sudden. I don't have to like her behavior to try to protect her. After all, I wasn't exactly a fan of Simon Reed, but I'm still trying to find his killer. I shouldn't have to remind you that we've searched for the murderers of some pretty unpleasant people in the past."

"No, I'm well aware of our track record together," Grace said. "How should we handle this?"

"You see if you can distract David, and I'll talk to Rosa," I replied.

"Wouldn't it be better the other way around?" she asked.

"I saw the way the man was looking at you. Trust me, he'd rather help you with an order than he would me."

"Seriously? I didn't notice anything."

"It was there. Believe me."

"Okay, if you say so," she said. "Let's go."

"Back again already?" David Clifton asked, clearly confused about seeing us again.

"I had a question about a bulk order," Grace said. "I'm the regional manager for a rather large cosmetics company, and we're thinking about changing suppliers for our office products. Do you have a minute to talk to me about it?"

"Absolutely," he said. The man was nearly drooling, whether from the prospects of a potentially big order or spending time with Grace, I couldn't say.

As they began to discuss the hypothetical order, I turned to Rosa. "I need some new pens for the donut shop. Could you help me while they're chatting?"

"Certainly," she said, pointing me toward the other side of the small shop, where I'd spotted them before.

Once we were there, I asked softly, "Rosa, do you need help?"

"I thought you wanted to buy some pens," she said, clearly confused by my question.

"I mean out of here. You're scared of him, aren't you? Grace and I can get you out."

She glanced over at her husband, who was lost in conversation with Grace at the moment. "No, I'm okay."

"Clearly that's not true. You're afraid of him, aren't you?"

"He's got a big heart," she said apologetically. "David would never hurt me."

"Can you be sure about that, though?" I asked. "He doesn't seem to be the type to forgive and forget adultery."

"Nothing ever really happened between Simon and me," she said, clearly backpedaling as fast as she could. "It was all just innocent flirting. I never would have gone through with it. I love my husband." The last line had been said with no conviction whatsoever.

"Are you sure that's the story you want to stick to?" I asked her.

"It's the truth. Why shouldn't I stand by it?"

"You asked us for help earlier, and don't try to deny it. I know that wasn't my imagination."

"I just don't want you to make him mad," she said. "Most times he's pretty good. Maybe I've overstated things. I have a tendency of being a little overly dramatic at times. He's a decent man, and in his own way, I know that he loves me."

"Is that reason enough to stay, though?" I asked her. I might not have approved of the way she'd dealt with the stress of her marriage, but that didn't mean that I wanted to see her living in fear, either.

"It's complicated," she said.

"It always is. So, is there anything we can do?"

"Yes," she said.

"All you have to do is name it," I replied.

"Leave here, and don't ever come back. You'll only make things worse if you stay."

"Are you sure that's what you want?" I asked her.

"I'm positive."

What else could I do? I walked over to Grace and said, "I'm sorry to interrupt, but I've got to get back to April Springs. Are you coming?"

"We're just about finished wrapping things up here," David said, clearly upset about having the proposed sale end so abruptly.

"Give me your card," Grace said. "I have to clear it with my boss, anyway."

"Fine, but I'd like your number for our records. Surely a woman in your position has a business card as well."

"You know what? I'm all out," she said as we walked toward the door. "I'll call you."

David was still frowning as we left, and we didn't slow down until we made it to my Jeep.

"What did she say?" Grace asked.

"She wants us to leave her alone," I said. "Grace, I tried to get her to let us protect her, but she clearly wasn't interested."

"What about her plea for help earlier?"

"She claims that she was being overly dramatic," I said. "What can we do?"

"I don't know, but I'm not giving up just yet," she said.

"We'll figure something out together," I said as I took off. "Where to now?"

"I've got a date with Stephen in forty-five minutes," she said. "Do you mind heading back to April Springs?"

"That sounds like a good idea to me. We've run out of people to talk to here, anyway. Where are you two going?"

"I'm not sure. He said it was going to be a surprise," Grace said.

We were within a mile of the April Springs city limit sign when I heard a siren behind me. I looked in my rearview mirror and saw lights flashing.

What had I done now? I wondered as I pulled over to see what was going on.

CHAPTER 12

"WAS I DOING SOMETHING WRONG, Chief?" I asked Chief Grant as he approached my Jeep window.

He leaned over and told Grace, "Your phone is off."

She pulled it out, and then she smiled. "So it is. You didn't have to pull us over to get my attention, though."

"Suzanne, would you mind driving to the donut shop parking lot? I need to talk to both of you."

"That sounds serious," I said, but it was to his retreating back. "Wow, he really doesn't like you to be out of touch, does he?"

"That's not what this is about," Grace said as I pulled out and headed for Donut Hearts.

"How do you know?"

"If I can't read him at least a little by now, I've been wasting my time going out with him," she explained. "If it were Jake, would you be able to tell what was on his mind by that exchange?"

"Not nearly as much as I'd like to," I admitted.

"You don't give yourself enough credit," she said.

"Maybe. I wonder what's going on?"

"I don't know, but we're about to find out. Maybe we should go inside so we can have some privacy."

"If we do that, I can guarantee you that someone is going to bang on the door and expect donuts," I told her.

"Seriously? It's way past your regular business hours."

"It doesn't matter if it were eight o'clock at night," I

explained. "There's something about a donut shop that some folks can't seem to pass up."

"I'd say that's in your favor, normally."

"Normally, but not always," I said. "We could always go back to the bench where we spoke with Emma last night."

"That sounds good to me," she said. We parked in front of the shop and made our way over. The chief must have gotten distracted by something along the way, because it was a good five more minutes before he drove up and parked beside my Jeep.

"Sorry about that," he said as he joined us. "Why aren't we meeting inside?"

"Suzanne doesn't want to sell donuts she doesn't have," Grace said. It made perfect sense to me, but the chief was clearly baffled by her explanation. Instead of asking for clarification though, he just shrugged it off.

"You two managed to stir up quite a bit of trouble in a short amount of time in Union Square."

"It's a gift, isn't it?" Grace asked him.

"I don't know about that. I got permission from the police chief to ask a few questions myself, and the next thing I know, I'm getting complaints that two of my citizens are going around getting everybody all riled up."

"Riled up? Really? All we did was ask a few simple questions," I said. "Who complained about us?"

"I don't know, and that's the truth, but even if I did, I'm not sure I would tell you. When you run your little investigations, you need to keep a lower profile, do you understand me? I hate getting chewed out, which is what I just endured, especially if I haven't done anything to merit it."

"Sorry," Grace said as she patted his shoulder.

"It might go a little farther with me if you sounded more sincere," he grumbled.

"I do the best I can," she said. "While you're here, I need you to look into something for me. Rosa Clifton is in an abusive relationship with her husband, and she wants to get out."

I had to say something at that point. "Grace, we're assuming a lot of things in that statement. We don't know that it's abusive, and when I asked Rosa if she wanted any help, she was most emphatic about turning us down."

"Because she was afraid of the repercussions," Grace said. At that moment, we both noticed the chief shaking his head. "What is it?" Grace asked him.

"The woman played you both," he said simply.

"What are you talking about?"

"I was there two hours ago, and when I walked in, she had her husband backed into the corner. She was terrorizing him about something, and for a second there, I thought I was going to have to pull her off of him."

"Maybe she finally got up the nerve to fight back," Grace said a little uncertainly.

"There have been three domestic disturbance calls to their home in the past nine months," the chief said. "Neither one of them would admit to anything, but according to their neighbors, Rosa was always the aggressor, never David. I read the reports. If Rosa got you two believing that she was the one in trouble, then she did a mighty fine job of acting."

I thought about our conversation with the man, and I realized that it was tainted more by Rosa's reactions than anything her husband had actually said or done. Could it be true? I prided myself on being able to read people, but if what Chief Grant was saying was correct, Rosa had gone out of her way to deceive us. But why would she do that? Was she simply trying to cover up her affair with the deceased, or was it something darker than that, say murder? And was her husband *really* the injured party? Everything the chief might have said could have been true about

Rosa being the aggressor, but that still didn't clear the man of murder.

"You're awfully quiet, Suzanne," the chief said, bringing me back to the moment.

"I'm just trying to reconcile what we saw and heard with what you're telling us," I said, not sharing every bit of my reasoning. After all, there was no point muddying the waters until we had more facts than we did at our disposal at the moment.

"I'm afraid that it's a fact of life. People lie all of the time," he said with a shrug. "I wouldn't try to read too much into it."

"Is that really how you feel, Stephen?" Grace asked him, clearly unhappy about his confession. "Do you just naturally assume folks are lying to you?"

"Unfortunately, more times than not, that turns out to be the case," he said.

"I'm not at all sure I like what this job is doing to you," she said simply.

He looked frustrated by her statement. "Grace, it's just the way things are. Spend a day in my shoes and you'll know what I mean."

"No, thank you," she said. "Suzanne, are you coming?" she asked as she headed back to my Jeep.

"Is that all you wanted, Chief?" I asked him.

The poor man looked thoroughly confused by what had just happened. "I don't understand what's going on here."

"If you don't know, I'm not going to explain it to you," Grace said. Then she turned to me. "If you won't drive me, I'll walk."

With that, she turned up the road to walk the hundred yards to her home.

"What about our date tonight?" he called out to her.

"I'm not in the mood to go anywhere tonight anymore," she called over her shoulder.

I started after her, but the chief put his hand on my shoulder before I could leave. "Would you try to talk some sense into her, Suzanne?"

"Hang on, pal," I said, releasing myself from his grasp. "Whatever issues the two of you are having are none of my business. I'm turning over a new leaf to try not to get involved in other people's lives so much." It was true, too, though I hadn't been very successful at it so far.

"I just don't understand women," he said wistfully as he watched her walk away.

"If it's any consolation, we don't always understand ourselves, either."

"No, that's no help at all," he said.

"Sorry," I answered, and then I headed for my Jeep and drove up the last bit of Springs Drive to Grace's house.

To my surprise, the chief followed.

Grace was just walking onto her front porch when we both pulled up.

"Hey, hang on a second," he said to her.

"Yes?" Grace asked coolly as she turned to face him.

"We need to talk."

"About?"

"Grace, are you *trying* to be difficult?" he asked. His youth showed a little for the first time in a long time.

That got a slight smile. "I really don't have to try that hard, do I?"

"Let me give you two a minute alone," I said as I started to get back into my Jeep. "Grace, I'll be up at the cottage when you're finished here."

"Suzanne, there's *nothing* we can't say in front of you."

I didn't want to be there, but I looked over at Chief Grant, and he nodded in agreement. It appeared that I was staying right where I was after all.

"Okay, you've got the floor, Chief," she said once that was settled.

"I know we're going through a rough patch right now, but don't give up on me," he said, his voice cracking a little as he said it. "I'm doing the best I can."

That softened her a little. "I know your job is taking its toll on you."

"That's no excuse, though. I'm going to be a better boyfriend. You deserve at least that much from me."

Grace started to tear up, and I was really starting to feel uncomfortable. It was a sweet moment, but it should have been between two people, not three. The best I could do was look away, but there was nothing I could do not to listen in on their very private conversation.

Grace walked to him, wrapped her arms around him, and planted a solid kiss on his lips. "You're doing just fine. I get a little needy sometimes, that's all, and when I see your heart start to harden, it worries me. I love you."

"I love you, too," he said. "I'll work on it."

"And so will I," Grace replied.

"What exactly are you going to be working on?" he asked with a hint of laughter in his voice. The tension was broken between them, and I felt a flood of relief. They were good for each other, and if they could find a way to work things out, I was cheering for them.

"I'll try to be a little more understanding. If you're still interested, I'd love to have that dinner we had scheduled."

I glanced over at him and saw that he was suddenly uncomfortable. "There might be a break in the case. Is there any way that I could take a rain check?"

"What kind of break?" she asked, now more concerned about his progress than the missed dinner opportunity at the moment.

He looked at her for a few seconds before he answered. "I probably shouldn't be saying this, but Theodore Reed took off this afternoon. A neighbor saw him packing his car in a hurry, and when he asked him what was going on, he said the man looked white as a ghost."

"Do you think it's related to his brother's death?" Grace asked him.

"It's never good when a suspect runs," the chief said. "Do you mind if we postpone our dinner? I have a few leads as to where he might be that I want to check out."

"Wouldn't he be long gone by now?" I asked, forgetting that I was supposed to be keeping a low profile.

He turned to me and answered, "There's a chance of it, but from what I've heard, he didn't have much money on him, and his bank account was nearly empty long before today. I have a hunch that he's holing up somewhere close."

"Go," Grace said. "We'll have dinner another night."

"Tomorrow?" the chief asked her, clearly eager to please her.

"Tomorrow would be great," she said, and then she kissed him soundly again. "Now go."

"We're good then?"

"We're better than good," she said. "We're great."

"Excellent," he said with a broad grin.

After the police chief got into his squad car and left, I said, "I'm glad you two worked things out, but I'm not sure I needed to witness it."

"I wanted Stephen to be able to express his feelings in front of you," Grace said. "It was good for him to do it."

"I'm not sure how good it was for me," I said.

She laughed, clearly feeling better about her relationship than she had in some time. "You'll get over it, I'm sure. Now that my evening has freed up, I have an idea."

"I'm listening," I said.

"Let's have one of our old-time slumber parties," Grace said. "We can make something with a lot of calories and not much nutritional value and watch an old movie like we used to."

I looked at my watch. "That sounds good to me, but you know I have an early bedtime, right? I've got to be up tomorrow morning to make the donuts again."

"That's fine by me," Grace said. "Should we do it at your place or mine?"

"We rarely do it here," I said. "You should get the honor of hosting once in a while yourself. If you don't mind me slipping out in the middle of the night, I think it sounds like great fun."

"I'm on board," she said. "Before we get started, let's run over to the grocery store and get some decadent treats."

"Is there anything in particular you had in mind?"

"I'm in the mood for triple chocolate cupcakes with milk chocolate icing and chocolate milk," she said.

"Wow, that's a lot of chocolate," I said, remembering the book club treat that I'd abandoned when my friends had left suddenly.

"Is that a problem?" she asked me.

"Not for me," I said. "I've been training myself for years in the art of consuming massive amounts of chocolate. I'm just afraid that you won't be able to keep up with me."

"In your dreams. I'm going to win this race. I guarantee it."

"It's not really a competition," I said with a smile.

"No, not with the way I'm going to beat you," she answered, laughing.

It was as though we were kids again, one trying to best the other, and I loved it. Being married to Jake was everything I'd ever dreamed of and more, but there were times like this that it was nice to revert to my teenage years and just hang out with Grace. Having her friendship over the years was a real gift, and I cherished it.

"What do you say?" she asked me.

"I say we go shopping, and then we start our own little bake-off."

CHAPTER 13

"MAYOR, WHAT ARE YOU DOING here?" I asked George Morris when I ran into him in the baking aisle.

"I go shopping, too, Suzanne," he said a little gruffly. "After all, a man has to eat."

"I just didn't peg you as a baker," I said, trying not to smile.

He frowned as he studied the cake mix in his hands. "I'm not. It's a special occasion."

"You're not moving before you try Charlotte out first, are you?" I asked softly. I wanted my friend to have a life, but I also wanted him to stay right where he was. I knew it was selfish, but I couldn't help wanting the people I cared about to stay in my life forever.

"No, at least not yet," he said. "Keep your voice down, okay? Nobody knows what I'm thinking about doing. Where's Grace?" he asked as he looked around the store.

"She's checking out the ice cream section," I said. "So, if you're not moving, then why the cake mix?"

"It's Cassandra's birthday tomorrow," he admitted. "I'm going down to Charlotte to tell her my plans, so I thought I'd surprise her with a homemade cake."

"George, have you ever baked a cake before in your life?"

"No," he said grumpily, "but I've been reading the directions. How hard could it be?"

"Harder than you realize," I said. "Grace and I are making cupcakes. Why don't you come by her place and we'll help?"

"I don't know. How would that look, the mayor hanging out with two attractive young women like that?"

I smiled and kissed his cheek. "Why, George, that might be the nicest thing you've ever said to me. I think you're handsome, too."

"Suzanne, stop that," he said, though I thought he looked secretly pleased by the kiss, as well as the compliment.

"Come on, it might even help your reputation," I said with a grin.

"It's really not as easy as it sounds?" he asked me.

"It's not bad, but there might be a tiny learning curve. Do you have a cake pan? They recommend a nine by twelve, but I like my eight by eight. Then again, most of the time I make cupcakes, and they are completely different."

"I have no idea what size my pan is," he said.

"Pan? As in you own only one pan? Seriously?"

"I've managed to limp along with it just fine so far," he said.

"Ah, but then again, you've never baked a cake before, have you?"

He nodded. "Point taken. Still, I don't want to interrupt your time with Grace. I know you two don't get that much of a chance to hang out together."

"Trust me, she'll love it," I said. "Now, let's get you a mix, some icing, and we'll handle the rest of what you'll need."

"I don't have oil or eggs," he said.

"We've got that covered," I told him as Grace came down the aisle.

Grace looked delighted to see the mayor. "Baking, Mr. Mayor?" she asked with glee.

I warned her not to tease him with a look, and she got it

immediately. "What do you think about helping George make a birthday cake for his lady friend?" I asked her.

"That sounds like fun," she said. "Have you got any candles? They have the kind that you can't blow out here."

"I'm not putting candles on Cassandra's cake at all," George said, pronouncing his judgment as though there was no room for discussion.

"Okay, but then how will she know it's for her birthday? Are you going to sing to her when you give it to her?"

George frowned. "Where are the candles? I want the regular kind that blow out, though. That's where I draw the line."

"They're right here," I said as I reached behind him and grabbed a box. "How old is she?"

"I'm not putting that many on a cake," George said. "One will do just fine."

"Okay," I said, knowing better than to tease him about it.

"How am I going to get the thing to Charlotte without ruining it? I haven't thought this thing through. Maybe it's not such a good idea after all."

"Come on, don't lose your nerve now," I said as I put my arm in his. "I've got a carrier at the cottage you can use that will be perfect."

"Okay, if you say so," he said.

"What kind of ice cream did you get?" I asked Grace, looking at the half gallon.

"Double chocolate chip," she said as she showed me the label. "What else do we need?"

"One of these, at least," I said as I grabbed a triple-threat chocolate cake mix for us, too. "There's no reason we can't bake too, is there?"

"None that I can think of," she said as she got some icing.

"Do you have eggs?"

"I'm sure I do," Grace said.

"Then let's go." George was still standing there.

"Are you coming?" I asked him.

"I don't really have much choice at this point, do I?" he asked.

"No, sir. I'm afraid your fate, at least for tonight, is in our hands."

"Is it *supposed* to look like that?" George asked as I pulled his cake from Grace's oven.

It looked fabulous to me, and the aroma filling the kitchen made me breathe in deeply to take it in in all of its glory. "What did you expect?"

"I don't know. I've never baked one before. Remember? Not that I'm sure I can claim that I baked this one. You two did most of the work."

"Nonsense. We were just acting in an advisory capacity," Grace said.

"Uh huh, sure," George said skeptically. "When can we taste it?"

"It's for Cassandra, remember?" I asked him.

"Oh. That's right. Got it." He looked disappointed to be reminded of it.

"We're not saving our cupcakes for a special occasion, and we bought the same mix you used. You have to hang around and join us for ours."

"I don't know. I've got to be up early tomorrow," the mayor said.

"Earlier than me?" I asked him with a grin.

"Suzanne, nobody gets up earlier than you do," he replied with a smile of his own. "Okay, I'm sold, but could I do more of the work on this one?"

"Why not?" I asked. After all, Grace and I would be watching him closely, and the mayor seemed intent on learning.

"Good," he said as he reached for another mixing bowl. After opening the box and cutting the plastic packet inside, he poured the mix into the bowl, but as he reached for Grace's last egg, his hand brushed against it, knocking it to the floor, where it promptly broke. "Blast it all," George boomed. "Look what I've done."

"And that was my last egg," Grace said glumly. "We should have bought more at the store."

"Don't worry about it," I said. "Need I remind the two of you that I live just up the road? I'll grab one and be back in a flash."

"You'd better make it two," George said. "With me, you never know."

"Tell you what. I'll bring whatever I've got in the fridge. That way you can break as many as you'd like."

Grace was wiping up the remnants of the cracked egg with paper towels. "I'm not sure I'd go that far," she said with a laugh.

"I can do that. After all, I made the mess," George said.

"Grab a few more towels and wet them. You can go behind me and wipe the floor, and then I'll follow you with dry ones."

"It appears that you two have this covered," I said as I headed for the door. "See you soon."

I walked down the now-dark road to my cottage and used my key to get inside. Flipping on a few lights, I marveled at how quiet the place seemed. Though Jake hadn't been gone that long, it was almost as though the cottage could sense his absence. I was being silly, and I knew it, but I couldn't do anything about it. I wondered how he was doing, so I reached for my phone to call him.

After a moment of panic, I realized that I'd left it on Grace's kitchen countertop.

The call would have to wait until I got back.

Going to the fridge, I was happy to see that I had seven eggs left in the carton that I'd bought a few days before. Even George should be able to get one good egg out of the batch.

Tucking the carton under one arm, I flipped off the lights as I walked out, stopping to lock up behind me on the way.

The carton started to slip, and I shifted suddenly to try to keep them from falling.

I hadn't even had a chance to grab them when someone hit me from behind, the carton of eggs crashing out of my grip and landing on the porch as I was shoved back into the door.

CHAPTER 14

I T TOOK ME A MOMENT to get my balance back, and when I finally turned around, whoever had hit me was long gone. My shoulder was aching, but it could have been much worse. If I hadn't felt the eggs slipping out of my grip at the last second, and if I hadn't pivoted around to try to keep them from falling, that blow would have hit me directly in the back of the head instead. I peered off into the darkness, but whoever had struck me was clearly gone. Why would someone attack me on my own front porch? It had to be because of the murder investigation! That meant that Grace and I had struck a nerve with one of our suspects, but which one? I reached for my phone again, and then I remembered where it was. Grabbing my keys, I unlocked the front door again.

I didn't immediately call the police, though.

I bolted the door behind me first.

After I told the chief what had happened, thankful that we still had a landline at the cottage, I phoned Grace. "Hey," I said.

"How long does it take you to get a few eggs, Suzanne? Did you forget why you were going over there?" she asked playfully.

"Somebody just attacked me," I said.

"That's not even funny to me, and we both know that I have a warped sense of humor," Grace said.

"I wish I were joking, but unfortunately, I'm not," I replied.

"You're serious? Is whoever did it still there? Are you okay?"

"Slow down. They're gone. My shoulder took the hit, but I'm afraid the eggs are broken."

"Forget the eggs," she said. "We'll be right there."

Before I could say another word, she hung up on me. Thirty seconds later, she and George were there, pounding on my front door.

It was good to have reinforcements on the scene.

George insisted on looking around outside, so Grace and I stayed out on the porch as he searched around the house with one of Jake's heavy-duty flashlights.

"Do you see anybody?" I called out from the safety of the porch, or what I had once thought of as a secure place, anyway.

"No," he said as a squad car came ripping up the road.

The chief was out in an instant, and before any of us could say a word, he had his gun out and trained on George's flashlight. "Drop it!"

"Chief, it's George," the mayor said as the light tumbled out of his hands anyway.

The chief put his weapon back in its holster. "What are you doing here?"

"Well, I'm not baking a cake," George said, trying to protect his reputation even in this situation.

The chief sounded a little odd as he replied, "Okay."

"George was helping us with something at Grace's place," I said quickly. "We ran out of eggs, and when I came up here to get some, somebody hit me from behind."

"With this, I'm guessing," George said as he picked up the flashlight, and then, using his clean handkerchief, he retrieved a long piece of tree branch.

"Unfortunately, we're not going to get any prints off that," the chief said. "Suzanne, are you sure you're okay?"

"I'm fine," I said as I rubbed my shoulder. "Those eggs saved me."

The chief looked even more perplexed than he had before. "I don't see how."

"I was about to drop them, so when I shifted to secure them, whoever hit me missed my head and got my shoulder instead."

"We should take you to the hospital and get you checked out anyway," the chief said.

As George nodded in agreement, I said, "No, thanks."

"What do you mean, no thanks? Something could be broken."

I moved my arm around, swinging it from the shoulder. It was a little stiff, and I knew it would be even worse in the morning, but I would still be able to function. "It's not, though. See?"

"Have you called Jake?" the chief asked.

"No, and I'm not going to," I said, coming to an executive decision on the spot.

"Suzanne," the chief said, "he's going to want to know."

"If I tell him what happened, he's going to rush right back here," I said.

"Is that a bad thing?" George asked.

"He's dealing with problems of his own right now. Besides, whoever did it is clearly an amateur at it. I don't think they'll try it again."

"What makes you think that?" the chief asked.

"Come on. What was the plan here? They didn't bring a weapon with them, and they didn't even know that I wouldn't be home. When the first strike missed my head, whoever did it panicked and ran away instead of sticking around and finishing the job. Do any of those things sound like a pro's work to either of you?"

"No, but we all know that amateurs can be more dangerous than professionals," the chief said.

"I'm not saying I won't be careful, but I'm not going to let this slow me down. If anything, it's proof that Grace and I are on the right track."

The chief turned to his girlfriend. "Can you at least try to talk some sense into her?"

"As a matter of fact, I think she's making perfect sense," Grace said. "It's going to be okay."

The chief shook his head in disbelief. "Think of me, then. How's Jake going to react when he finds out that I didn't tell him his wife was attacked? He'll skin me alive."

"Me, too," George said. "At least think of us."

"Tell you what. I'll tell him tomorrow, when things have calmed down a little."

"What about in the meantime?" the chief asked. "You can't stay here alone. That's where I draw the line."

"She's staying with me at my place," Grace said. "Remember?"

"For tonight," the chief reluctantly agreed.

"For as long as she needs to," Grace answered.

I wasn't sure how I felt about everyone's need to protect me, but I knew if I pushed back too hard, one of the men was going to call my husband. Ordinarily I would have loved to have Jake there, but I'd meant what I'd said. I was in no immediate danger, and he had some serious problems he was working through with his family. "Okay. I give up. Grace, thanks for making room for me."

"Are you kidding? I'm going to love having company."

"Good. That's settled then," I said as I reached down to pick up the dropped carton. "Hey, there's still one good egg left. We can make those cupcakes after all."

"You're still going to bake after what just happened?" George asked me incredulously.

"Are you kidding? It's even more reason. Grace and I are clearly on the right track. We just need to narrow things down a little now."

"Maybe I should postpone my trip to Charlotte," George said.

"And miss Cassandra's birthday? Not on my account you're not," I said. "Since there's nothing left for us to do here, what say we reconvene at Grace's place? I just need to grab a few things from inside if I'm moving in with Grace for a few days."

As I started to go inside, I found three people following me.

"I'm perfectly capable of doing this alone, you know," I told them.

"Maybe so, but you're going to have company, whether you like it or not," the chief said.

I decided not to fight them on it.

Honestly, I was just as happy to have them there. I might have talked bravely about the attack, but it had shaken me up more than I cared to admit.

I knew that we were dealing with a dangerous character, but now it was personal.

Apparently whoever had killed Simon Reed was now coming after me.

"Comfy, Suzanne?" Grace asked me once I was settled into her guest bedroom. The men had gone, but not before the chief had warned us that he'd be sending his staff to patrol around Grace's home as often as he could manage it. It had been the only way George would agree not to do it himself, so we'd finally accepted the chief's offer of unofficial police protection.

"You bet," I said. My shoulder was sore, and hurting more by the minute, but I wasn't about to complain about it. After all, it could have been much worse.

"Are you sure you don't want to call Jake?" she asked timidly.

"Now don't you start on me," I said. I knew I was pushing my luck by not calling my husband, but I wanted to see what tomorrow would bring. If we still hadn't made any progress by the next night, I'd probably let him know what had happened. I wasn't sure how I was going to deal with it if he called me the next day, but I figured I'd burn that bridge when I got to it. "You know what? I'm really not all that sleepy. Do you mind chatting a bit?"

"Are you kidding? That sounds great to me. What do you want to talk about?"

"Take a wild guess. Who do you think attacked me tonight?"

"As a matter of fact, I was just thinking about the same thing," she said. "Clearly we have someone worried about us. I wish I had as much confidence in us as your attacker appears to have."

"Let's go through them one by one and try to figure out where we stand," I said. "Who's first on our list in your book?"

"Sherry West comes to mind," Grace said. "She doesn't really seem like a planner, does she? She's more than a bit of a hothead, too. Whoever attacked you clearly didn't come prepared. Do you think ambushing you was really a last-minute decision?"

"The choice of weapons seems to dictate it," I admitted, "though if we're dealing with a really clever killer, they may have just wanted it to look like it was a spontaneous act of aggression."

"Do any of our suspects really seem that devious to you?" Grace asked.

"If the chief is right and Rosa was playing us from the start, she could do something like that," I said. "Then again, her husband could have done it himself."

"Do you think so?"

"It's a possibility. What better way to get rid of a rival than by framing his wife for the crime? He could eliminate two problems with one violent act," I said.

"But why would he go after you?" she asked.

"I don't know. Maybe he thinks we know more than we really do."

"That wouldn't be too hard, given the fact that we don't know all that much," Grace answered.

"We know more than you're giving us credit for," I said. "In a relatively short amount of time, we've come up with a pretty impressive list of suspects, and we've uncovered motives for all of them."

"Excluding Barton, Emma, and her parents, right?" Grace asked me.

"I'm sorry, but I can't bring myself to think of any of them as a killer, but even if I could, can you really imagine one of them trying to attack me from behind? I know that I can't."

"We both know that frantic people can commit desperate acts when they're pushed hard enough," Grace replied softly.

I looked at her oddly. "Does that mean you believe they are still in the running?"

"I just don't see how we can rule them out," she said.

I was still thinking about that when my cell phone rang. Was it Jake? Grace was about to excuse herself when I saw that it was Sharon Blake, Emma's mother. "Don't go anywhere," I said, and then I answered, "Hello?"

"Suzanne, I hate to do this to you, but Emma and I will both be missing work tomorrow."

"What's going on?" I asked.

"We've been sitting here in the living room talking to several friends for the past two hours trying to figure out what to do about this mess. Barton could be in serious trouble, and Emma, Ray, and I have been calling everyone we can think of trying to come up with a way to keep him from going to jail."

"You're worrying too much. Nobody's going to jail just yet," I said.

"Listen, we know you're friends with Chief Grant, and Grace is dating him, but we're concerned that he's going to try and railroad Barton into this."

"Hang on a second," I said. "Is Barton with you now?"

"Yes, he's been here all evening," she said.

"And he's never left?"

"No, we thought it would be better if he stayed with us. He and Emma have had their heads together since three. Ray came home after five, and we've had a steady stream of folks in since then."

I could hear people chatting in the background, which confirmed at least that part of her story. "That's good to hear."

She sounded perplexed when she answered. "I don't know why you would say that."

"Someone attacked me less than an hour ago," I said. "That clears all of you."

"Suzanne, why would someone come after you? Are you okay?" she asked.

"My shoulder's a little sore, but other than that, I'm fine."

"I still don't know why anyone would attack you." Just as suddenly, she added, "Never mind. Obviously whoever did it is worried that you're going to catch them." After a moment's pause, she added, "We were all on your list of suspects." I started to speak when she interrupted me. "Don't bother denying it. I can't even say that I blame you."

"We have to consider every possibility," I said, feeling suddenly bad about what Grace and I had been discussing so recently.

"Nobody's going to fault you for that. I'm sorry we're abandoning you tomorrow. I suppose if you really need me, I can make it in."

"Don't worry about it. Remember, I usually work one day alone anyway. I'll be fine."

"Are you sure?" she asked.

"I'm positive. Give Emma my love."

"I will."

"Sharon, do me a favor. Don't let her know that any of you were on our suspect list at any point, would you?"

She paused longer than I thought she needed to when she answered. "That depends."

"On what?"

"Would you tell your mother, if our roles were reversed?"

She had a point that I couldn't deny. "Of course I would. Forget that I even asked."

"I thought you'd understand," Sharon said.

After I hung up, I said, "Barton, Emma, and her folks are all in the clear. They were with neighbors and friends for the past three hours, so none of them could have done it."

"Attacked you, you mean," Grace said.

"Surely you don't think the attack was unrelated to Simon Reed's murder?" I asked. "That's too big a coincidence to swallow."

"You're right," Grace said. "Sorry. You know how I get when I'm in killer-hunting mode."

At that moment, her doorbell rang.

"I'll be right back," she said as she stood to get it.

"You're not answering that door alone," I said as I got out of bed and threw on the robe that I'd brought with me from home. "I'm coming with you."

"Suit yourself," she said.

"Do you have any weapons on hand?" I asked her.

"That depends. Do you count pepper spray?"

"I count whatever can help stop another attack," I said.

After Grace armed herself with the canister from her purse, we went to the door as the bell rang again. Grace peeped out, and then she tucked the spray into her pocket.

"Who is it?" I asked.

Just as I spoke, I heard Momma's voice clearly from the other side of the door. "Ladies, let me in this instant, or I'll find a way to knock this door down myself."

CHAPTER 15

AFTER GRACE UNLOCKED AND OPENED the door, I looked at Momma and smiled. "Were you really going to try to break the door down?"

"Do you even have to ask?" she asked me as she rushed up and hugged me. The pressure on my shoulder didn't feel great, and I must have winced a little from the pain. Momma pulled back and studied me carefully. "Suzanne, you are really hurt, aren't you?"

"I'm going to have a whale of a bruise in the morning, but I'm going to be fine other than that," I explained.

Phillip, who'd been standing just behind his wife, asked, "You didn't get a glimpse of your attacker?"

"No, I got hit from behind. The force of it pushed me against the door, and by the time I got my wits about me and turned around, whoever had done it was gone."

"Jake is on his way, I presume," Momma said.

"As a matter of fact, he is not," I answered. I could see her starting to protest, so I cut her off. "Momma, he's dealing with his own issues. Besides, I'm fine."

"You need to call him," she said. It was clearly more of an order than a request.

"If I haven't made any progress tomorrow, I'll tell him then," I promised.

She looked at me sharply. "Is that a promise?"

"I'm not in the habit of lying to my mother," I said.

"How about the time you slipped out of your window and shimmied down the tree to meet Greg Bascomb in the park?" she asked me.

"Momma, I was in the eighth grade. Surely the statute of limitations on that has run out by now."

"My dear, sweet child, when it comes to mothers and daughters, there *is* no statute of limitations," she said.

Phillip touched her shoulder lightly. "Dot, it's late, and unless I miss my guess, Suzanne is going to be getting up soon to make donuts. Let's leave the girl in peace."

"You seem awfully cavalier about my daughter's well-being," she said fiercely.

Before he could answer, I hugged her, which effectively shut her up. "Momma, he's right. I need my sleep. Besides, the chief is going to be sending a patrol car out here whenever he can. I'm safer here than I would be at the cottage."

"Perhaps," Momma said. She turned to Grace and asked, "Are you all right with accepting this danger as well?"

"Hey, nobody attacked me," Grace said.

"Yet," Momma added.

"Don't go getting her riled up," I said. "We're going to be fine. I promise."

"I don't know how you can fulfill that particular promise, but fine. We'll leave you two in peace."

After they were gone, I wasn't in any mood to go back to bed. "Why don't we sit up out here a little?" I suggested.

Grace glanced at her clock. "I'd love to, but Phillip was right. You're getting up soon."

"I can spare a few more minutes," I assured her. "I'd like to talk about our suspects more. Maybe it will help me get to sleep."

"Sure. Why wouldn't it? The folks who count sheep are really missing the boat, aren't they? Let's discuss murder suspects."

It was clear she was being sarcastic, but I wasn't going to let that distract me. "Okay. Besides Sherry, we've got the husband-and-wife team of Rosa and David Clifton. I can see either one of them doing it, but at least we know they didn't conspire to do it together."

"How do we know that?" Grace asked.

"Can you honestly see that pair cooperating on *anything*?" I asked.

"No, now that you mention it, I can't. Let's see. That leaves us with Clint Harpold, Theodore Reed, and Shalimar Davis, besides Sherry. They each had their reasons, didn't they?"

"Theodore was having a fight about money with his brother, and don't forget, it appears that he's on the run right now, which can't be good. Clint could have been jealous of Simon and killed him in a rage, and Shalimar is volatile enough to be capable of bursting into a fit of anger at a moment's notice, based on what we've seen and heard."

"So, what should we do with our final six suspects?" Grace asked me.

"Tomorrow, as soon as I finish up with Donut Hearts, I say we press each and every one of them except Theodore. We might just have to leave him up to the police. In the meantime, we start implying that we know more than we do and see where that gets us. I have a feeling we've got the killer spooked. If we push them hard enough, somebody's going to snap."

"Wow, that sounds like a dangerous game we're about to play," Grace said.

"Any objections?" I asked her.

"Not from me. I *like* living on the edge." She glanced at her clock again. "I hate to break this party up, but if you're going to get any sleep at all, you'd better hit the hay."

As I stood, I heard a noise on the front porch.

The only problem was no one rang the bell.

Clearly whoever was there didn't want us to know that we were onto them.

"Whoever is out there had better run. I've got a gun this time," I said loudly.

"I hope you're lying," I heard a familiar voice say. "But just in case you're not, don't shoot. It's only me."

I opened the door and found my stepfather looking sheepish. "I didn't mean to scrape the chair on the porch floor. You weren't even supposed to know I was out here."

"What are you doing, Phillip?"

"I'm standing guard until morning," he said.

"I told you both before. We don't need protection."

"Suzanne, what's it going to cost you? Your mother is worried about you, so I volunteered to stand guard duty."

"But you won't get any sleep," I protested.

"I don't need nearly as much as I used to," Phillip said. "Besides, it will give me a good excuse to take a nap in the morning after you're safely at Donut Hearts."

"I'm not going to be able to talk you out of this, am I?" I asked.

"You know your mother. How many arguments have you ever won with her?" he asked wryly.

"You could count them on one hand and have several fingers left over," I admitted. "At least come inside."

"No, ma'am. I can't be a preventative measure if they don't know I'm out here," he insisted. "Besides, it's a nice night. I'm looking forward to a little peace and quiet."

"Unless they come back," Grace said.

"I doubt they will, but if they do, I'll be ready for them," he said as he showed us his holstered weapon. "I used to be the police chief around here, remember? I think I can handle an amateur with a stick."

"What if they come back with something a little more threatening this time?" I asked. I didn't want Phillip hurt on our account, even if he was there protecting us.

"I'll be ready for them," he said, slapping his holster gently. "Don't worry about me. Now go get some sleep. I'm going to want some donuts after we're finished up here," he said with a grin. "Dot told me as a reward I could get any three donuts I wanted without recrimination. That's how I'm going to stay alert all night, pondering my choices."

"Okay, if you're sure," I said as I reached up and kissed his cheek. Grace did the same thing on the other side, and when we took a step back, the man was actually blushing.

"Go on now, you two," he said abashedly.

"Okay," I said.

"Thanks for looking out for us, Phillip," Grace said.

"The truth of the matter is that there's no place I'd rather be," he said.

Once we were inside and the door was locked, I had to admit that I felt better about the situation. After all, what could it hurt having Phillip outside? I didn't think the killer was coming back, but why take the chance? If Grace and I were still stymied by five the next evening, I was going to call Jake and tell him everything. I didn't need a man to protect me, but his presence would be welcome regardless. I prided myself on my independence, but only a fool wouldn't take help when it was offered, and I knew that Jake would die for me just as surely as I would die for him.

I had no trouble getting to sleep, and when I woke up the next morning, I found a note from Grace on the kitchen table.

"*Suzanne,*

I got the afternoon off, so I'll be by the donut shop when you close. Until then, stay out of trouble!

If you can. Hahaha.

Grace"

I left a little addendum to it.

"Grace,

What can I say? Trouble seems to follow me around.

See you later, and thanks for investigating this murder with me.

*Until we find the killer, we **both** need to watch our backs!*

Suzanne."

I walked out of the house and found Phillip smiling at me.

"How was your night?" he asked me.

"Better than yours, I'll bet," I said. "How did you manage to stay awake all night?"

"That's the thing. It's not all night yet," he said after checking his watch.

I glanced back at the closed door. "I feel bad about leaving Grace exposed like this."

"Don't be. I'm going to the shop with you, and once you're safely inside, I'm heading back over here. I've had my fair share of stakeouts over the years, so what's another all-nighter to me?"

"You really are great for doing this," I said as we walked down the darkened street. I felt safer being with him, though I hated that Grace was unguarded, even if it was only for a few minutes.

"All part of the friends and family protection service," he said. "It's a nice night, isn't it? By the way, how's your shoulder doing?"

"It's a little stiff," I admitted as I tried to flex my arm a little. It was going to make things tougher at the shop, especially since I'd be working alone, but I'd manage. I always did.

"Keep moving it," Phillip said. "That's the best way to get it to loosen up."

As we neared the shop, I turned to face him. "Am I crazy not calling Jake right away?"

"That's your business, Suzanne. I make it a point not to get in the middle of anyone else's marriage if I can help it."

"That's probably a good idea, but I'd still like to know your opinion. Is Jake going to be upset when he finds out I withheld this from him?"

Phillip took a moment to consider my question before answering. "He might get upset for a little bit, but I think he'll understand. Suzanne, he knew what kind of woman he was marrying from the start, so it's not as though this should come as a shock to him."

"I can't tell. Is that a good thing, or a bad one?" I asked as we neared the Donut Hearts front door. I was relieved to see that at least the shop appeared to be fine. A part of me had been worried that I'd find the front window shattered, or the door kicked in, but it looked normal enough to me, at least as far as I could see.

"It's a good thing, as far as I'm concerned. You want to handle this on your own. I can respect that, and I'm sure that Jake will, too."

"But am I really handling it myself? I didn't call Jake, but you stepped in, and if you hadn't, I'm sure the mayor or the police chief would have."

Phillip didn't even have to think about that. "Asking for help, or accepting it, is not a sign of weakness, at least as far as I'm concerned. Sometimes it just makes sense to take a hand when it's offered to you."

"I know, but it's hard, isn't it?" I asked as I pulled out my keys.

"It's pretty close to impossible," he said with a grin. "Let me go in first, okay?" he asked as I unlocked the door and opened it.

"Fine, but don't ask me to stay out here alone," I said,

glancing around at the shadows, especially those coming from the park across the street.

"I wouldn't dream of it," he said as he pulled out his weapon. It was easy enough searching the donut shop, and soon enough, his handgun was back in its holster. "Everything checks out here. Are you going to be okay being here alone all day?"

"No worries," I said. "I can handle it. After all, I do it once a week anyway."

"Maybe so, but not after just being attacked on your own front porch," he said. "I'm sure if you ask your mother, she'd be glad to come over and keep you company."

"Thanks for the suggestion, but I'm good," I said. "Hadn't you better be getting back to Grace's front porch?"

"I'm on my way," he said. "One thing. If you see anything suspicious, call Chief Grant, even if you feel foolish doing it. It's better to be safe than sorry."

"Yes, sir, I will," I said. I gave him a nice hug, which he seemed to appreciate more than the kiss I'd given him earlier with Grace, and soon enough, he was on his way back to her place.

I locked the front door behind him, took three steps, and then double-checked it once, twice, and then a third and final time. If someone got in, they were going to have to make a ruckus doing it.

I had the jitters at first, but as I started into my routine, flipping on the coffee pot out front and the fryer in back, my nerves started to settle down. By the time I'd dropped all of my cake donuts, I was back in full donut-making mode, lost in the art and the craft of what I did for a living. Besides, I didn't have a whole lot of time to dawdle and dwell on what had happened to me the night before. There were dishes to wash and yeast donuts still to make. I was going to have my hands full, but I didn't mind.

Maybe it would allow me to put the trauma of what had happened to me in the past.

Being obsessed with my donuts was something that would work in my favor, and I decided to take advantage of every last minute of it.

CHAPTER 16

I THOUGHT ABOUT STAYING INSIDE DURING the break I had coming to me as the yeast donuts went through their first rise, but in the end, I decided that I was just being foolish. I needed that time away from the shop, even if it was only a few steps. It helped me focus on the tasks still ahead of me and forget any troubles that I might have had earlier.

At least it was relatively warm.

I knew cool and then cold weather would be coming soon enough to April Springs, and Emma and I would be bundling up when we took our breaks, but at the moment, there was just enough of a pleasant breeze, and very little humidity, to make the night air just about perfect. As I sat there, I thought about how much my life had changed since I'd divorced Max and bought the shop. It was amazing how much I'd retooled my entire existence in such a short period of time, but that was my norm. I'd think long and hard about a decision before I made it, chewing it over and dissecting it from every angle, but when I was ready to move, it was always done with great speed and confidence.

I was smiling about just that thing when I suddenly saw movement across the road beside the bookstore.

At first I thought it was simply a shadow, but then it began to creep steadily out of the darkness and get closer and closer to the light. Whoever was stalking me was clearly unaware of the configuration of lighting and greenery around them. They might have been under the impression that they were being stealthy, but I knew better.

At least I'd brought a heavy ladle with me. It might not have looked like much, but I was willing to wager that it would be effective if I used it against someone. I owed whoever had attacked me a headache at the very least, and I planned to return it with interest.

I stood up from the outdoor chair, but instead of going into the shop, I walked out onto the street, swinging my ladle as I did so. "I'm not afraid of you. Come out of the shadows and take the beating you so richly deserve."

Whether my words or my actions prompted the stranger in the shadows to move I had no way of knowing, but there was a sudden release of air, and whoever had been stalking me darted off into the woods.

What they didn't know was they were on my home turf now. I knew those woods from ages and ages of playing in the park, and nobody was going to lose me in those trees.

Only they did.

I wasn't sure how they managed it, but I couldn't find them, something I would have bet was impossible just minutes before. I had a choice to make. In my haste to take the ladle weapon from the kitchen, I'd forgotten to take my phone. Cursing myself for leaving it behind a second time, I turned suddenly and made a mad dash for the donut shop door. I expected at any second to feel a hand reach out and grab my shoulder, and as I put the key in the door lock, it took everything in my power not to turn to see if the stranger had decided to come after me yet again.

I got inside and slammed the door shut, locking it in place before it really had a chance to settle back into its frame.

As I looked back into the park, I could swear I caught a

glimpse of a face, but then again, it could have just been wishful thinking on my part.

Had I really just spotted Theodore Reed, the victim's brother and current fugitive, or had my imagination just supplied his face because I'd wanted to see it so badly?

Either way, I couldn't just stand there.

I had to call the chief of police and rouse him from his sleep. I felt badly about doing it, but really, what choice did I have? If I had really seen Theodore Reed lurking in the shadows, the police chief needed to know, and the sooner the better. However, if I'd been mistaken and the man was nowhere to be found, I could live with the embarrassment.

After all, finding the killer was all that counted at the moment.

I started to dial the chief's familiar number, but it took a second for my hands to stop shaking long enough for me to do it.

"Yes? What is it, Suzanne?" the chief asked groggily. I'd clearly just woken him up.

"Someone's lurking outside the donut shop," I said. "Can you send someone over here?"

"I'll be there myself in three minutes. Are they still there?"

"No, I was outside, and when I spotted them and shouted, they took off," I admitted.

"Toward the park or downtown?"

"Toward the park," I replied. "I chased them, but they got away. You know what? Forget it. Whoever it was is probably long gone by now."

"We don't know that, though. See you in a minute."

After he hung up, I peered out the window, searching for some sign that anyone was still out there.

I couldn't see a thing out of the ordinary, and I wasn't about to go back out again for a closer look.

Two minutes later, the chief drove up, but instead of coming straight to the shop, he used the powerful light on the side of his car to scan the park, the bookstore, and the open areas around Donut Hearts. He drove at a crawl, but I couldn't see anything out of place from where I was watching.

Five minutes later, he pulled up in front of the shop.

I unlocked the door and let him in. "You didn't see anything, did you?"

"Not yet," he said. "Stay here, okay? I'm going to search on foot."

"Alone?" I asked him. He'd pulled on his uniform, but it was clear he was still tired from lack of sleep. Here I'd been worrying about him being too stressed, and I'd just added more to his plate.

"I've got more officers coming," he said.

"I shouldn't have called you."

"You did exactly the right thing. Now, don't you have donuts you should be making?"

"Yes, but I'd rather watch what you're doing."

"It's not going to be all that exciting, especially if whoever was out there is really gone. I'll call you when we're finished."

Chief Grant went back to his car as two other squad cars approached, and before the three officers started searching on foot, he gave them a set of instructions. As they fanned out, each one armed with a heavy flashlight and a service revolver, I did as the chief had suggested. My yeast donut dough needed my attention.

As I worked on rolling out the dough and using the aluminum cutter wheel to pop out neat rounds and holes, I wondered why Theodore would come to my shop in the middle of the night. Was he there to attack me, or was he trying to warn me about who the real killer was? If it was a simple warning, why hadn't he come forward when I'd walked toward him? Or had he just panicked when he'd seen me? I wasn't sure I was ever going to get the answers to my questions, but I hoped the chief and his people at least found some evidence that someone had been over there. Otherwise I was going to feel pretty foolish.

My cell phone rang, and I grabbed it before it could ring more than once. "Did you find him?"

"Let me in," he said.

"Okay, but I need to know," I said as I hurried out of the kitchen toward the front.

He was frowning when I got to the door. "There was no sign of anybody out there," the chief said as I opened up.

"Not even a footprint or cigarette butt ground into the dirt?" I asked.

"It's been pretty dry around here lately," he said. "I wasn't expecting to find any indications someone was out there, but we looked. I'll say one thing. You're probably right. Whoever was out there is long gone by now."

"But you do believe me, right?" I asked, eager to have him acknowledge that I wasn't losing my mind.

"I'm sure you saw someone there," he said. "If you say it was Theodore Reed, then that's what I'm going with."

I recalled how dismal the view had been from where I'd stood. "Well, *someone* was there. I thought it was Theodore Reed, but I could have been wrong," I admitted.

"We'll keep a lookout either way. Shouldn't you have help here by now?" he asked as he looked around.

"Emma and Sharon are both spending time with Barton," I said.

"Can you do this alone?"

"I already manage it one day a week," I said. "I'll be fine."

"Sure, making donuts you've got down cold, but what about being alone? Maybe you should call Grace."

I laughed at the suggestion. "Trust me, having her here at this time of the morning wouldn't be doing either one of us any favors. She offered, but I was smart enough to decline. I'll be fine."

"I'm sure you're right, but don't open early, okay? I'll have someone swing by a little before six to check on you."

"Did you know Phillip was guarding Grace's place?" I asked him.

"Yes. He ran it past me earlier," the chief admitted.

"And you approved?"

"I didn't see any reason the chief shouldn't do it," he admitted as he took in a deep breath.

"Care for some coffee and a treat while you're here?"

Chief Grant appeared to consider it before shaking his head. "I'd better not. If I'm lucky, I'll get a little more sleep before I have to go into the office."

"I'm really sorry I woke you," I apologized.

"Nonsense. You did the right thing. Promise me one thing though, okay?"

"What's that?" If he was going to suggest that I give up my investigation, I was going to have to decline, but I'd do just about anything else if it helped make his life easier.

"Don't do anything foolish."

"I was thinking about making Caffeine Bomb Donut Holes a little later," I said with a grin. "Is that what you meant?"

"I'm not sure why you'd want to do it, but bake away. Just keep your doors locked until six."

"I can do that," I said, "but you know, the bad guy can just waltz right in after I open for business. I can't very well sell donuts and coffee through a slot in the door."

"I'm well aware of that fact, but there's no reason to tempt fate."

"Agreed," I said. "Thanks for coming by."

He tipped a hat he wasn't wearing. "Just serving and protecting, ma'am."

"Go home, Chief," I said with a smile.

After he was gone, I felt better than I had all morning. I was still alone, but just knowing that other people were out there watching over me gave me a sense of well-being that I embraced. The rest of my donut-making duties went smoothly, and by the time I opened for business, I was ready to face the world. I'd been kidding about the new cake donut, especially since they had been done by the time I suggested it, but maybe I'd give it a shot someday. I wasn't a huge coffee fan, but I knew that many of my customers were. Maybe I could combine some espresso into the mix or find some other way to juice the donuts up. I'd have to discuss it with Emma on another day, but for now, it was time to open the shop.

I glanced back at the displays and was happy with the way everything looked, so I unlocked the front door and waited for my first customer to show up.

CHAPTER 17

I WAS SURPRISED TO FIND THAT my first customer of the day was a woman who had never come into the donut shop alone before since I'd known her.

"Elizabeth, are you all right?" I asked my book-club friend when she walked into the shop. She appeared to have been up all night, and I was getting more concerned about her well-being by the minute.

"I'm as good as I'm going to get, given the circumstances," she said. "I came by to apologize to you."

"You have nothing to apologize for," I said. "I'm worried about you."

"You're going to have to get in line," she said. "Jennifer and Hazel are giving me so much support that I can barely breathe." She must have realized how that sounded, because she quickly added, "Not that I don't appreciate it. I'm just not sure there's anything anyone can do at this point. You're divorced, aren't you?" she asked me timidly.

"I've since remarried, but yes, my first marriage fell apart in a rather spectacular manner," I admitted. "It was tough going for a while, but I managed to get through it. I know it's probably not going to mean much to you at the moment, but I've never been happier than I am right now. It took everything I went through with Max to help me find Jake."

"From what I've heard, he's one of a kind, though," she said sadly.

"He's unique in his own way, but there are good men still out there," I said. "First you have to deal with your situation, though. Is there any hope to save it?" I wasn't about to suggest she leave her husband. I didn't know anything about her relationship with him, so I didn't feel capable of giving her even basic advice.

"I honestly don't know. There's something he's hiding from me, and it's tearing us apart," she said, her voice turning into a whimper.

"Is it another woman?" I asked.

"I don't think so. Suzanne, I don't know what to do. Hazel and Jennifer are suggesting that we all take a trip together. They think if I can get away for a few weeks, I might be able to get a little perspective on the situation. You couldn't break away too, could you?" she asked as she glanced around the empty donut shop.

"I'm sorry. I wish I could, but it's just me at the moment, and I'm not sure when my assistant is even coming back. If the shop closes for even a day or two, I'm not sure I could ever recover from the financial loss."

"I understand completely," she said. "Still, I thought I'd ask."

"I would have been hurt if you hadn't," I said as I gave her a hug. "Can I at least get you something to eat and drink while you're here?"

"Thanks, but my appetite isn't much these days," I said.

"Not even a bear claw?" I offered.

"Well, maybe I'll take one with me," she conceded.

I bagged two up for her, just in case she found her appetite again. As she reached for her wallet, I said, "These are on the house. When are you all leaving on your trip? Do you have any idea where you're going?"

"Jennifer is planning it, with some help from Hazel. I'll be in touch when we get back."

"I'm counting on it," I said.

As Elizabeth walked to the door, she turned and stared at me for a second. "I'm glad I've got you as a friend," she said. "You're good for me."

"I feel the same way about you. Have a lovely time."

"I'll try," she said.

After she was gone, I found myself remembering what it had been like finding Max and Darlene together. It had been a blow I wasn't sure I'd ever be able to recover from, but I'd found my way back. Having Momma, Grace, and my other friends and family helped pull me through the darkest of times, and I cherished them all for the parts they'd played in my recovery. I was sad I couldn't go with the ladies on their trip, but I knew that Jennifer and Hazel would do their best to help Elizabeth, and I hoped that she knew she could count on me, too. Sometimes it was easy to forget the darkness after it was over, but I knew that without my experience of getting through what had felt like a string of insurmountable obstacles at the time, I wouldn't have been ready to let Jake into my heart later. I hoped my friend found her true joy again, no matter if it was with her husband or from a brand-new chapter in her life.

"Rosa, what are you doing here?" I asked an hour later as Rosa Clifton came into Donut Hearts. "Is your husband with you?"

"He thinks I'm at the beauty parlor," she said. "It was the only way I could get away."

She was trying to play the victim again, but after what the chief had told us, I wasn't swallowing it this time. "You can drop the act. I'm not buying it anymore."

"What act?" she asked me in an offended manner.

"We spoke with the chief of police. You've been cited for disturbing the peace on three separate occasions, and your neighbors have backed your husband's side of the story every single time."

Rosa processed the information in less than a second, and when she looked at me again, her expression had changed to one that was decidedly more reptilian in nature. "They never could mind their own business."

"At least you're not denying it," I said, glancing down to see if I had anything I could use to defend myself. Had Emma moved my baseball bat from under the counter like she'd moved my dough cutter, or had it just been pushed to the back? Either way, I couldn't get it without alerting her to what I was doing.

"Relax, Suzanne. I'm not here for a confrontation, so you can stop reaching for the gun you keep under the counter."

"It's a baseball bat, actually," I said.

"Really? I would have taken you for a gun nut, given your husband's former occupation."

"You know about Jake?" I asked her, troubled by her statement on several different levels.

"Do you honestly think you and Grace could come around questioning me and I *wouldn't* investigate you and your family?"

I liked the sound of that even less, but it was time for a little brashness on my part. Why was the donut shop always deserted when I needed witnesses and/or reinforcements around? "Then you know that my husband was a top-notch investigator for the state police."

"The key word in that sentence is 'was,'" she said. "You need to stay away from me and my husband. Am I making myself clear?"

"And if I don't?" I asked.

"You won't like the outcome," she replied, and I didn't doubt it for one second.

"Why are you so eager for us to leave you alone, anyway?" I

asked her. "Are you afraid we're going to discover that one of you killed Simon Reed?"

"Please. We had nothing to do with his death," she said.

"And I should believe you why, exactly?"

"Because I'm telling you that it's the truth," she said.

"Then why the warning? You weren't in April Springs last night around eight by any chance, were you?"

She looked at me oddly, as though she couldn't understand why I was asking the question. "Not that it's any of your business, but we were both in Charlotte last night. Someone wants to buy the shop, and we were there for meetings until late into the evening."

"Why should I believe you?"

"At this point I don't really care what you believe," she said. "The thing is that the new buyer doesn't want anything to do with the murder, so if you and your little pal keep digging into our lives, it could hurt us financially."

"And we wouldn't want that now, would we?" I found the only way to deal with most bullies was to get up in their faces. Sometimes that earned me a punch in the snout, though.

"Trust me, we wouldn't."

"I suppose there's someone who can verify these meetings," I said.

"Of course there is, but if you're expecting me to give you a name and a number, you're even crazier than you appear to be, which is saying something. Why is a donut maker digging into this, anyway? It's not like you had any real connection to Simon."

"It happened back there," I said, pointing to my kitchen. "That makes it my business."

Her harsh expression seemed to soften for a moment. "I can see that. But you're barking up the wrong tree with us. We didn't kill him."

"How can you be so sure that your husband didn't do it? After all, he admitted being there at the pop-up bistro the night of the murder."

"Because I saw him leave!" she said loudly.

"Funny, but you wouldn't admit that before. Why the change of tune?"

"I wanted to see him try to squirm his way out of it," she confessed. I had no trouble believing that she'd done exactly that, but I still couldn't take her word for it.

"I still need some kind of proof about last night before I drop it."

"Call the Marriott on Park Road," she said. "We reserved a meeting room there, and we even had dinner served to us. Is that good enough?"

"Not yet, but it will be once I get confirmation."

"You don't trust anybody, do you?" she asked me harshly.

"Oh, there are some people I trust. You just aren't one of them," I said, keeping my gaze directly focused on her.

"You know what? I'm tired of dealing with you. Do as I say, or face the consequences."

"I won't be scared off," I told her.

"Then we're finished talking. As long as you leave us out of this, we're okay, but the moment you try to drag us back in, I won't make any promises about your future well-being."

"Neither will I," I said.

After she was gone, I looked up the hotel's number in Charlotte, and after some cajoling, I got them to admit that Rosa and David Clifton had indeed been there in one of their conference rooms having a meeting. I hated crossing their names off our list since they seemed to be such attractive suspects, but I couldn't let my bias against them keep me from acknowledging that, barring some kind of stealth transportation device, they couldn't have made it to April Springs and back to Charlotte without their absences being noticed. That didn't necessarily mean that neither of them had killed Simon Reed, but I couldn't believe that the attack on me the night before hadn't been committed by the murderer. It was just too big a coincidence to swallow.

Unless I learned something contradictory, the Cliftons were going off my list, but that still left Grace and me with a healthy set of suspects that were all still viable candidates, including Sherry West, Clint Harpold, Shalimar Davis, and of course, the missing Theodore Reed.

CHAPTER 18

T HE REST OF THE MORNING passed quickly enough, especially given the fact that I was doing everything in the shop, from waiting on customers, cleaning tables, and trying to wash a dish and a coffee cup now and then so I could continue serving my customers. I really missed having an extra set of hands, but then again, I couldn't begrudge the Blake family for rallying around Barton Gleason. Phillip had come by as promised and made his selections. Grace had left for work, and he was on his way home for a well-deserved nap.

Still, by the time eleven rolled around, I was more than happy to lock up. Twenty minutes later, up to my elbows in soapy dishwater, I heard someone knocking on the front door.

"We're all out of donuts," I called out as I rinsed my hands and grabbed a nearby towel.

"That's a shame, but that's not why I'm here," Grace said. As I unlocked the front door to let her in, she asked, "Are you sure you can't scrape *something* up for me? I didn't have much of a breakfast, and I'm starving."

"We could always go back to Napoli's before we start investigating again," I said as I made my way back to my dirty dishes.

"I will waste away before then," Grace said melodramatically. "Not even a crumb for a poor, hungry soul?"

"I might have something for you," I said as I flipped a box open that contained eleven donuts in a mixed variety.

"You are a saint," she said as she zeroed in on a cherry cake donut. "Any chance there's coffee, too?"

"Sorry. The last pot just went down the drain," I said. "I can offer you chocolate milk or regular. Take your pick."

"Regular," she said. "Don't bother, I can serve myself."

"I wasn't going to," I said with a smile. "How was your short day of work?"

"I hate dealing with drama," she said. "Two salespeople are going at it like cats and dogs."

"Competitors can do that sometimes," I said.

"It's nothing like that. They're both on my team. I warned Gregory and Samantha that dating was a bad idea, but they wouldn't listen. Now that they've had a bad breakup, they are constantly trying to undermine each other in my eyes, and it's driving me mad. Any advice?"

"Me? I have all I can handle myself at the moment," I said as I pointed to the dirty dishes still waiting for their baths.

"Your problems are simpler than mine are," she said with a frown.

"That's why you make the big bucks," I said with a grin. It was true, too. Grace made a staggering amount of money compared to what I brought in on a daily basis, but I wouldn't have traded places with her for anything. I may have had my own difficulties from day to day, but they were mine, and I was in no rush to trade them for anything worse.

"True," she said. "Do you need a hand?"

"It would speed things up if you dried," I said, "but don't feel obligated."

"Say no more," she said as she grabbed a clean, dry dishrag and started working right beside me. As we polished off the stack, we shared a few pleasant memories from our childhoods that we shared after I brought her up to speed about my conversation with Rosa Clifton and the stalker I'd seen outside in the shadows, and before I knew it, everything was clean.

"Is that it?" she asked.

"I still need to make the deposit out, if the register balances."

"I may need to eat another donut, if that's the case," she said.

"Be my guest," I said, grabbing a cinnamon cake donut on my way past her.

"Hey, I was going to eat that," she said.

"You snooze, you lose," I replied with a laugh. "Do you want to know something? It tastes even sweeter knowing that you wanted it, too."

"Grow up," she said as she grabbed an old-fashioned cake donut from the box.

"You first," I said as I stuck my tongue out at her.

She replied in kind, and we both started laughing.

Fortunately the books all balanced, and in ten minutes, the bank behind us, we were on our way back to Union Square in my Jeep.

"So, where are we going to eat?" Grace asked me. "Napoli's again?"

"Down, girl," I said. "We need to speak with our suspects, at least the ones we can find at the moment, so that means it's got to be the Lazy Eye."

"I'm game if you are. If the main courses are anything like the desserts, it's going to be awesome."

"Remember, we need to push Clint and Shalimar about the murder, and about where they were last night as well."

"How's your shoulder feeling today?" Grace asked.

"It's stiff, it's sore, and there's a bruise that's getting bigger by the minute, but at least they missed my head, so I've got that going for me, anyway."

"Whoever thought chocolate cupcakes would save your life," Grace said with a smile.

"Or more precisely, a partial carton of eggs."

"I'd rather think of it as the chocolate treats," she replied.

"Fine. What do you think of what I saw outside the shop this morning? You believe me, don't you?"

"Suzanne, I *never* question you. If you say you saw Theodore Reed out there, then that's who you saw," Grace replied. There was no doubt in my mind that she was sincere. "What do you think he wanted with you?"

"I wish I knew," I said. As we pulled up in front of the restaurant, there were quite a few more folks there than there had been on our visit the day before. "Looks like they've got a crowd."

"If you can call seven cars a crowd," Grace said. "Look at the wave of people coming out," she added as she pointed to the door.

Sure enough, nearly a dozen people left at the same time. "Let's see what's going on," I suggested.

After we stepped out of the Jeep, I approached a woman in her forties as she was unlocking her car door. "Ma'am, we're not from around here. How's the food there?"

"Take my advice. Go to Napoli's, or go without. This place is terrible."

"Really? We heard the desserts were outstanding," Grace said.

"Yes, if all you want is pie or cake, but don't order anything else. The man uses salt as though it were a weapon."

"Is that why everyone else is leaving?" I asked as I pointed to the folks already getting into their cars and driving away.

"They had a lunch meeting," she said. "I wasn't eavesdropping, but it was kind of hard not to hear them arguing. Evidently the guy in charge was offended by the suggestion that he could use some cooking lessons. I thought there was going to be a fistfight for a minute. Anyway, enter at your own risk. The only thing saltier than the food is the waitress, or maybe the cook."

"Thanks," I said as Grace and I started to go in.

"You're actually going to give them a shot after what I just said?" the woman asked, clearly dumbfounded by our behavior.

"What can I say? We like living dangerously. Besides, we happen to love pie and cake," I said.

"I'll grant you that it's good, but it's not good enough to put up with those two attitudes," she said. "Good luck. You're going to need it."

"Thanks," I said as I gave her my best idiot's smile and waved.

She was still shaking her head as she drove off.

"She thinks we're morons," I said.

"Can you blame her?" Grace asked. "How do we do this? Are we really just having pie for lunch? I had donuts at your shop. I was kind of hoping for something a little more substantial."

"We're not here to eat, Grace," I reminded her.

"Well, not just to eat," she said.

"True. Tell you what. Sherry West is working at Baxter's. We'll grab some real food there."

"Maybe," Grace said as we reached the door. "Have you ever seen that place?"

"No. It's some kind of bar that serves food, right?"

"That will work as a loose definition," she said, "but I might just take my chances with the Salty Dog here."

"It's the Lazy Eye," I corrected her.

"As if that was somehow better," she said.

We walked in to find Shalimar bussing tables. "Did we just miss the lunch rush?" I asked her sweetly.

"If you can call it that." She lowered her voice as she added, "If I were you, I'd stick with the dessert menu again."

"Thanks for the tip," I said.

I glanced at Shalimar's arm where the sleeve was pulled up

153

and saw several scratches on her forearms. "What happened to you?"

"This? It's nothing. A stray cat was hanging around back by the dumpster and got a little aggressive with me," she said as she pulled the material back down to cover the marks. "What can I get you?"

"Do you have any carrot cake?" Grace asked.

"Sure. It's one of Clint's specialties."

"Make mine apple crisp pie," I said, and then I turned to Grace. "We can split them, if that's okay with you."

"It depends on how good the cake is," she said, and then she turned to Shalimar. "Didn't I see you in April Springs early this morning before sunrise?"

"What? No, I haven't been there in months."

"You mean besides the opening of Barton's pop-up bistro, right?" I asked her.

"Sure, besides that, I mean. Why do you ask?"

"I was out for a late-night walk, and I could swear that I saw you around 4 a.m.," Grace said.

"Lady, the only place I'm ever at four in the morning is home in bed. You must have been mistaken."

"My mistake," Grace said as we took our old seats at the counter.

"I'll be right back with your desserts."

Once she left us, I said, "Subtle, Grace. When have you ever been up at four yourself?"

"I'm sure it's happened at least once in my life," she said. "Do you believe her?"

"I don't see any reason not to. When she comes back, we need to hit her a little harder."

"What did you have in mind?" Grace asked me.

"I'm not sure. Let me think about it."

I didn't have long to ponder our next move. She was back

quickly with our desserts. It appeared that we'd both chosen wisely. If they tasted anywhere as good as they looked, we were in for a pair of treats.

"Shalimar, I think it's brave of you coming into work today at all," I told her as she delivered our dessert main courses.

"What do you mean? Why shouldn't I be here? I know it's not much, but it's better than being unemployed."

"You know, with the rumors and all, it takes a confident woman to show the world she doesn't care what anyone says or thinks about her." I was winging it, but I had a vague notion about where I was going with it.

Shalimar's fake smile quickly vanished. "Who's been talking about me, and what are they saying?"

"I heard a rumor that there's a witness that saw you follow Simon into the donut shop just before he was murdered," I said.

"Who said that? Whoever it is, they're lying."

"The police are being very hush-hush about it, but I understand they're bringing their witness to the station in April Springs this evening at six," I said. "In fact, in order to keep anyone from seeing them, they're stashing them at the donut shop where Simon was murdered to make sure nobody followed them there."

"How do you know that, if it's supposed to be such a big secret?"

It was a fair question, and I was trying to come up with a believable answer when Grace interrupted and provided one for me. "My boyfriend's the police chief, and he told me in confidence."

"Well, I don't have anything to worry about, since I didn't kill Simon." She walked over to the counter as she shouted, "I'm on break, Clint."

"Again? Shalimar, are you *ever* planning to actually waitress here?"

"Ha ha. Very funny. As a matter of fact, the more I think about it, I believe I'll take off early. I'll see you tomorrow, if the place is still open, that is."

She headed for the door without looking back at us once. Maybe we could use her extended absence in our favor. Clint walked out and seemed surprised to see us there. As he rolled his shirt sleeves down, I saw that he'd scraped his arm, as well as his hands. He must have seen my glance. "Shalimar asked me to help her with a stray cat out back yesterday. No good deed goes unpunished, right? How are you ladies doing? Skipping the main course and heading straight to dessert again?"

"Is there a better way to eat a meal?" I asked him. After I took a bite of the pie, I meant every word of it. It was truly amazing. "You're a pastry chef at heart, aren't you?"

I wasn't sure how he'd react to my comment, but as he slumped back against the wall, I regretted saying it. "That's what everyone keeps telling me, including my customers. What's the use? I'm not good enough, and I don't think I ever was."

"I don't know about your entrees, but if you ever opened a bakery, I'd be there every day, and I run a donut shop," I said. I wasn't even trying to boost the man's morale. His treats really were that good.

"That's nice of you to say, but I'm not sure I could make a go of that, either. I can't stand the hours. Can you imagine what kind of masochist gets up at two or three a.m., every day, day in and day out?"

"It must be tough," I said, trying to bite my tongue before I said too much. "I can't believe you're open today."

"I was here yesterday, and if things don't fall completely and utterly apart in the interim, I'll be here again tomorrow. Why are you so surprised?"

"It's just that we heard a rumor about you," Grace said, not wanting me to have all of the fun misleading our suspects.

"What rumor is that? Trust me, it's not true. Do you honestly think I would ever sleep with Sherry *or* Shalimar? I wish people would stop saying that I dated either one of them."

"We were talking about you being seen with Simon just before he was murdered," Grace supplied. "Evidently someone spotted you following him into the donut shop where he was murdered."

"That's a lie," he said rather strongly. "I never went near that place!"

"Well, it will all be cleared up tonight," I said. "They're bringing the witness to the donut shop this evening at six before they take them into the station to make sure no one's following."

"Well, whoever it is isn't going to give them my name, unless they're trying to set me up for murder," he said. "Listen, finish up your desserts, but then I'm closing early. Suddenly I don't feel like working."

"We can always take them to go, if you'd like," I offered.

"That would be great. Tell you what. I'll just charge you for one."

"We'll take it," Grace said. "Charge her, and make mine the free one."

"Seriously?" I asked her.

"Hey, I'll split the bill with you anyway," Grace replied.

In two minutes, our treats were boxed up and we'd paid our bill. Grace had started to leave a tip when Clint said, "Don't bother. She didn't earn it."

Grace couldn't bring herself to do that, though, so she put a pair of quarters on the counter anyway.

"Suit yourself," he said as he stuck them in the tip jar, a large bowl that was mostly empty. "Thanks for coming by."

"You bet," I said.

We got into the Jeep, and I drove around the corner, tucking it in behind a monster truck that had been jacked up to the sky.

"Are we finishing our treats here and now?" Grace asked.

"No. I want to follow Clint and see where he goes," I said.

"Good thinking," Grace said as she looked in the bag holding our treats. "Hey, he forgot silverware."

"Check the glove box," I said. There were a few takeout plastic utensils there, and napkins as well. There wasn't much of a selection since the Jeep was fairly new, but I knew there had to be enough to get us through our culinary crisis. "I doubt you'll have time to do more than take a bite or two," I warned her.

"I don't know about you, but that's all I need." I finally relented and took the offered spork, digging into the pie. Before I could put the bite into my mouth though, Clint drove out of the parking lot. I shoved the bite into my mouth and started the Jeep up.

"Where do you think he's going in such a hurry?" Grace asked me as I risked getting a ticket following him down the road. The man was clearly in a hurry to get somewhere.

"I have no idea. Home, maybe?"

"I doubt he'd be in that big a hurry," I said.

After five minutes, Clint had parked and left his vehicle.

Could it have been just a coincidence that he'd driven straight to the bar where Sherry West worked? I highly doubted it.

The two of them clearly had a connection in all of this, and I was determined to find out exactly what it was.

CHAPTER 19

"LET'S GO SEE WHAT THEY'RE up to," Grace said barely a moment after I'd come to a stop.

I jumped out on my side, and in one second we were heading to the bar. There was a dumpster close to the front door. Seriously? If it weren't a health code violation, it was, at the very least, a violation of common sense. We were nearly to the door when I saw it begin to open. I glanced inside and saw Clint turned and talking to Sherry.

Grabbing Grace's arm, I pulled her behind the dumpster.

"Hey!" she protested.

"Shh," I said as I pointed to the situation we'd nearly walked into. "They're coming out."

The smell was even worse when we crouched down, and I was suddenly sorry for every bite of dessert I'd had that day. At least we hadn't had a full meal at lunch. There was no way I would have been able to keep that down.

"Clint, enough!" Sherry said as she jerked her hand away from the chef. "I'm not taking one more step with you until you tell me what this is all about."

"They're on to you, Sherry," Clint said. "Two busybody women came by the café just now and told me that someone saw you follow Simon into the donut shop right before he was murdered."

"They actually said that?" Sherry asked, sounding angry

enough to live up to her redheaded reputation. "They mentioned me by name?"

"Well, no, but come on. You can be honest with me. You killed him, didn't you? Don't worry. I'll protect you."

Her gaze was as cold a one as I'd ever seen in my life as I peeked around the dumpster. "Why are you doing this? You can drop the act, Clint. It's obvious that you have wanted to be with me for years, but why did you have to kill Simon? We were on our way out. If you would have just waited a week or two, you could have acted on your feelings without killing someone!"

"I didn't kill him!" Clint snapped at her.

"Well, neither did I!"

"And besides, what makes you think I want to be with you?" Clint asked indignantly.

"Really? Now that the playing field is wide open, you're going to start acting that way? I'm not blind, Clint. I see the way you look at me."

"Lady, have you ever got it wrong," Clint said. "I came here to warn you, not to woo you."

"Get lost, you creep," she said, pausing only long enough to slap his face before she stormed off back inside the bar.

"I can't believe that just happened," Clint said softly to himself. "Let her hang, then. I did what I could to protect her from herself."

Clint walked back to his car, and once he was out of sight, Grace asked me, "Should we follow him?"

"I'm not at all sure what good it would do," I said. "It's clear he thought Sherry was the killer and just as obvious that she thought he did it."

"Do you think *anyone's* going to show up at the donut shop at six?" Grace asked me.

"Most of the bait we dangled is gone," I admitted. "Still, it wouldn't hurt to hang out there and see what happens." I'd

The Donut Mysteries: Cherry Filled Charges

used the method to lure a killer out into the light before, and hopefully it would work again. Besides, what else could we do at that point? I was beginning to wonder if we'd ever solve this murder. "We might as well head home."

"Fine by me," Grace said. "If it gets me away from this dumpster, I'm all for it. I'm not even hungry anymore. Hey, it just occurred to me that we never had a chance to ask Sherry if she was in April Springs this morning."

I thought about going inside the bar, but I'd suddenly had my fill of murder suspects and questioning sessions. "If it's all the same to you, let's save that for another time. Right now I want to just forget about murder, at least for a little while."

"I know just how you feel. You've had a long day, and the night isn't going to be a short one. Do you want to head back and try to take a nap before the six o'clock appointed hour?"

"Would you mind?" I asked her, suddenly feeling the weariness not only of the investigation but of running Donut Hearts by myself all morning.

"I've got some paperwork I can do at home. Can you nap at my place?"

"I'm happy to bunk there at night, but if it's all the same to you, I want to head back to the cottage. I'll be safe enough there during the daytime."

"I'm not sure about that," Grace said after biting her lower lip for a moment or two.

"Well, that's the great thing about being an adult. I don't have to ask anyone's permission to take a nap whenever and wherever I choose."

"Okay, I get it," Grace said, laughing. "You need a little alone time, though why you'd ever want to be away from me is beyond all comprehension."

"I know. It's crazy, right?" I asked with a smile. "Will you be okay without me?"

"I can always find something to eat once I get my appetite back," Grace said happily.

"I wasn't talking about food," I said.

"Suzanne, when are we *not* talking about our next meal? That's one of the things I love most about our relationship," she answered.

"Me, too. That, and your sparkling personality, of course."

"Of course," Grace said, and then after a long pause, she added, "Right back at you." After another moment of hesitation, she added, "I paused too long, didn't I?"

"A little bit," I said with a grin, "but that's okay. I forgive you." I glanced at my dashboard clock and said, "Let's meet up again at four."

"Do we get to eat at the Boxcar before our stakeout?" she asked me. "I'm sure I'll be hungry by then."

"Sure," I said, doing my best to contain my laughter. Maybe she was right. Maybe what we discussed mostly was our next meal.

It was still better than talking about murder.

An hour later, after a brief nap on my own couch and a quick shower, I was ready to face the world again. In my opinion, naps for grown-ups were highly underrated.

"Are you ready to eat?" I asked Grace when she answered her door.

"When am I not ready for that?" she asked. "Have a nice nap?"

"You bet. What did you do?"

Grace grinned at me. "I decided to take one myself. You're right. I do feel better."

"Would I steer you wrong? Now let's go grab something to eat so we can set up our stakeout in time."

"I'm ready if you are," she said, and then we headed over to the diner on foot. I didn't want the presence of my Jeep to spook anybody, and besides, taking the shortcut through the park was quicker than if we'd driven, if you added parking into the mix.

"What are you two doing here?" I asked as we spotted Phillip and Momma at the Boxcar.

"I had a sudden craving for cobbler," Phillip said as he pushed the empty bowl in front of him aside.

"Did you have ice cream with it?" I asked him as we joined them without waiting for an invitation first.

"I think it should be against the law not to," he said with a grin. "If you're in the mood, the peach is excellent today."

"Thanks, but we're both actually tired of dessert," I said.

"Suzanne, I don't know about Grace, but we need to get you to the hospital immediately. Something is clearly very wrong with you," Momma said with a fake stern expression.

"If you'd had the day we've had, you'd understand," I said. We'd stopped and chatted with Trish at the front and ordered two deluxe cheeseburgers, fries, and Cokes, one of my favorite combos to get there.

"What have you two been up to this afternoon?" Momma asked us once we were seated.

"We've been baiting a trap, and in about an hour, we'll see if we catch anything," I explained.

"I presume you're using yourselves as the lure," she said with clear disapproval in her voice.

"Not really," I said. By the time I finished explaining our plan to them, Trish brought our food and slid the plates in front of us.

"Thanks, Trish," we said in unison.

"Wow, it's almost as though you were twins," she replied

with a grin. "Phillip? More cobbler? Come on, you know you want it."

"Stop teasing him," Momma said. "He's had enough, and he knows it."

"As much as I hate to admit it, she's right," my stepfather agreed. "That doesn't mean that it wasn't delicious, though."

"You don't have to tell me. I've had seconds myself."

"With ice cream, I hope," Phillip said.

"Do you even have to ask?" Trish asked with a smile. She slid the check under his bowl and then took one out and put it between Grace and me. "Holler if you need anything."

"You bet," I said, and Grace and I dug into our meals. The first bite of burger was its own nirvana. Trish had found a local supplier for grass-fed beef, and her deluxe burgers had gone up a dollar with the change. Some folks had howled about the price increase, at least until they tasted them.

I thought the new version of burgers was worth more than she was charging, but I wasn't about to mention that to her.

"Who is supporting you?" Momma said as she waited for me to finish a bite.

"I'm a grown woman, Momma. I know the donut shop doesn't make much, but it's enough to get by on."

"I'm talking about this evening," she said with a frown.

"She knows that, Dot," Phillip said as he grinned at me.

"I know that she knows," Momma said. "Is the chief going to be with you? Or has Jake made it back early, by any chance?"

"We're not trying to capture a killer," I said. "We just want to see if anybody shows up. We'll tell the chief if we get any results."

"That's not sufficient," Momma said.

It was clear she was about to further scold us when Phillip spoke up. "Dot, I'd be more than happy to go with them."

"This is getting to be a habit for you, watching out for us, isn't it?" I asked him.

"I just thought you could use some company," Phillip replied. "Dot has a business dinner this evening, so I'm just going to be by myself anyway."

"I told you that you were welcome to join us," Momma answered.

"No, thanks. When you start haggling over prices, my eyes start glazing over, just like yours do when I tell you about a crime from two centuries ago. Just because we're married doesn't mean we have to enjoy everything the other one does."

"I'm well aware of it," Momma said as she suddenly stood. "Since you're going to all be in good hands, I'll leave you to each other."

"Don't go away mad, Momma," I said.

"I'm not angry, dear child. I'm just in a rush."

"Hey, that one's ours," I said as she grabbed both checks.

"Too late," she said with a grin, and then she leaned over and gave her husband a quick kiss. "Don't wait up for me."

"I'll probably be on guard duty again tonight," he admitted. "After we see if the trap is sprung, I'm planning on heading home and catching a nap before I take up my post again."

"It's really not necessary," I said.

"I know that. I *want* to do it; I don't feel as though I have to. Let an old retired cop feel useful again, would you?"

"Don't look at me, Suzanne. I sleep better knowing he's out there myself," Grace said.

Her answer surprised me. I hadn't realized that she was worried, so I certainly wasn't going to run my stepfather off until things settled down.

"Be that as it may, I hope you are all careful," Momma said, and then she was gone.

"I really was going to pay for our meal," I said after she'd left the diner.

"Sometimes it's better just to sit back and let it happen," Phillip said. "Now, where are you going to wait for the bad guy? You're not actually going to be inside the donut shop itself, are you?"

"I thought we might," I admitted.

"If it were me, I'd talk to Paige and see about putting two chairs near the front window of the bookstore. You've got a clear view of Donut Hearts from there, and you're out of the line of fire in case things get ugly."

"What about the back of the donut shop?" I asked.

"That's where I'll be," he admitted.

"I'm not about to let you take all of the risks of my plan."

"Fine. We can trade places. I just thought you might like the AC."

"Grace and I will wait far enough behind the shop to be in the trees there beyond the parking lot. If we see anything, we'll call you."

"Makes no difference to me," Phillip said.

Grace grinned at him. "That was your plan all along, wasn't it?"

"No, ma'am. I'm still happy to take either point."

"Just don't get caught up reading, mister. We might need you," I said, realizing that if my stepfather found a book of old crimes, he might be no good at all to us.

"It's a deal," he said.

Once we were headed out the door, I told Trish, "Here's your tip."

She refused the money. "Your mother already took care of that, too."

"Of course she did," I said as I put it back in my pocket. I turned to Phillip. "You're right. Sometimes it's best to not even put up a fight."

"That's been working out for me so far," he said as he glanced at his watch. "You two better take up your positions, and I'll head over to Paige's place."

"Let us know if you see anything suspicious," I said.

"You do the same."

Once we'd split up, Grace said, "I still think he's getting the better part of the deal."

"That's fine with me. If someone's going to make a move, they'll probably do it in back anyway."

"Do you really think this is going to work?"

"What do we have to lose at this point?" I asked.

As we were walking to our post, I saw the mayor approach on foot.

"Give me a second," I said to Grace. "I need to chat with George."

"I'll be back in the woods somewhere," she said as she pointed.

"Don't worry. I won't be long."

"You're back soon," I told George. "How was Charlotte?"

"It's a wonderful city, full of vibrant life and lots of new experiences, and anyone should be thrilled to have the chance to live there," he said.

"Is that you talking or Cassandra?" I asked him.

"They are her words," he admitted.

"So, what did *you* think?"

"There are too many people, too many cars, and not enough trees," he said. "I can't do it."

"I'm sorry," I said as I stroked his shoulder. "Are you okay?"

"We didn't break up, Suzanne. She's coming up here next week to give small-town living a try. If that doesn't work out, maybe she'll end up commuting. I'm not letting her go that easily."

"Good for you," I said.

"What are you two up to?" he asked me.

I didn't want to get into explaining our trap. There just wasn't time. "I'll tell you tomorrow," I promised.

"That sounds as though there's a story there." Instead of pressing me on it, though, he nodded. "I can't wait to hear it later."

As he walked away, I said, "For what it's worth, I'm glad you're staying."

"So am I," he said with a grin. "Thanks for the advice."

"What are friends for?" I asked as I headed off to rejoin Grace on our stakeout.

By seven, we realized that our trap had failed. I was about to call Phillip when I saw him sneaking through the woods toward us. "Time to throw in the towel?" he asked us softly.

"I guess so," I said. "Oh, well."

"Suzanne, just because it didn't work doesn't mean that it wasn't a good idea."

"Thanks. Are you heading home?"

"I am, but I'll be by Grace's place in a few hours," he said.

"Thanks for backing us up and standing watch over us," I told him.

"Yes, thanks so much," Grace echoed.

"You are both quite welcome. See you soon."

We left our hiding spot together, and as Phillip headed to the cottage he shared with Momma on foot, Grace and I started off for her place.

"What now?" she asked me.

"We spend the evening coming up with a new plan," I admitted.

"You said you were going to call Jake tonight, remember?"

"I know," I said, not wanting to recount the attack to him and then having to explain why my phone call was coming nearly twenty-four hours later. "Can we go to your place and get something to drink first?"

"You're not just putting off the inevitable, are you?" she asked me with a grin.

"Of course I am," I said with a shrug.

"Good enough. I just wanted to make sure that you knew it."

"Oh, I know it better than you do. Do you have anything cold and icy to drink at home?"

"I've got a few things that might work for you," she said with a smile.

"Any chance one of my choices is lemonade?"

"No, but we could always make some. I've got sweet tea, though."

"That sounds good, too," I said. "Though the time it took to make fresh lemonade would at least postpone the phone call a little longer."

"Suzanne, put on your big-girl pants and make the call."

"After I get something to drink, I promise, I will."

CHAPTER 20

I TOOK MY SWEET TEA OUT onto the back deck so I could call Jake in private. I wasn't particularly excited about what I had to tell him, but what choice did I have? My aching shoulder reminded me that whoever had killed Simon Reed wasn't playing around. I knew that Jake would take the assault personally. I just hoped that he wouldn't be angry that I'd held the information back from him for so long.

Maybe it would go to voicemail and I'd be spared telling him immediately.

As I put my tea down on the top rail of the deck, a nail poking up that I hadn't seen cut my wrist in a long, straight line. It was deep enough to draw blood, though not much. I grabbed the paper towel I'd wrapped around the glass to keep the condensation off my hand and dabbed at the blood. It hadn't been a deep jab, but it had still left an angry scratch four inches long. I was relieved that I wouldn't have to get a tetanus shot. I'd needed one the year before after stepping on a rusty nail in the park.

And at least it allowed me to delay my call a little longer.

I went back inside.

"That was quick. Didn't he answer?"

"I never got a chance to call," I said as I showed her the angry line on my wrist. "Do you have any disinfectant?"

"Did you get that from my railing? I'm so sorry. I've been meaning to have it fixed, but I keep forgetting. This is all my fault," she said as she got a small first aid kit from one of her kitchen drawers.

"I should have seen it. I guess I was a little preoccupied."

"I feel so bad," she said as she sprayed the wound. "Do you want a Band-Aid?"

I looked and saw that it had drawn very little blood, and it had already stopped bleeding. "No, I think I'm good. At least I got a tetanus shot last year." I saw the look of concern on her face. "Grace, I'm fine. Really. I do worse things to myself in the donut shop every week."

"Yes, but this was on my property. If you want to sue, I'm okay with it."

I had to laugh. "I think I'll live. Now, if you'll excuse me, I'm going to call Jake."

"Are you sure you're okay?" she asked me, clearly still upset about the incident.

"It's nothing more than a scratch. Would you stop apologizing?"

"I can't help it. At least let me buy you a treat to make up for it."

"What did you have in mind?" I asked.

"I don't know. How about more ice cream?"

"That sounds great," I said, and then I added, "You know, the cold cup might help ease the pain of my gash after all."

"It's nowhere near being a gash, Suzanne," she said with a laugh.

"That's what I keep telling you," I said. I went back outside and decided to make that call after all.

Just my luck, my husband picked up on the second ring. "Hey, stranger. I was wondering if I'd hear from you today. How goes the case? Are you two making any progress?"

"Some," I admitted. "How are things there?"

"I'm heading home," he said with a sigh. "I should be there in an hour."

"Is that a good sigh, or a bad one?" I asked him.

"I've done all I can for the moment. We'll talk about it when I get home. Distract me while I'm driving. Tell me what's been going on there."

I gave him a brief summary of what we'd been doing, and then I hesitated a moment before telling him about the attack the night before.

He was too good an investigator not to pick up on the pause. "Suzanne, what are you not telling me?"

"Something happened, but the important thing to remember is that I'm fine," I said, trying to calm him down before he had a chance to get too concerned.

"Now I'm really worried. Talk to me."

"Grace, George, and I were making chocolate cake last night at Grace's place. George broke her last egg, so I came over to the cottage to grab ours."

"Do I even want to know why you three were having a bake-off?"

"It's not important," I said. "Just let me tell this, okay?"

"Okay," he said.

"Anyway, everything was fine until I was leaving the cottage. I was locking the door behind me when the egg carton started to slip. I leaned over to grab it, and somebody hit me from behind."

"What? Are you okay?"

"I just said that I was," I told him. "Don't get worked up about this, Jake. It's okay."

"Who did it?" Those three simple words, one short sentence, held more malice in them than I'd ever heard my husband use before. I pitied my attacker if Jake ever found them.

"I don't know. They hit my shoulder instead. It staggered me, and by the time I turned around, whoever did it was gone."

"What did they use?"

"Chief Grant found a large branch near the cottage," I said.

"Hang on a second. The chief knew about this?"

"Naturally. I had to call him, didn't I?"

"Sure, why bother letting your husband know what was going on," he said, clearly unhappy about being the last one to know.

"You were busy with Paul, Jake. Don't be mad."

He took a few deep breaths, and then he said, "I'm not angry with you, Suzanne. I just wish you'd called me."

"What would you have done if I had?"

"I would have broken every traffic law getting to you last night," he admitted.

"I knew I'd be fine," I said. "The chief had patrols come by all night. I stayed with Grace, and Phillip stood guard on the front porch the entire time. He even walked me to the donut shop this morning. In fact, he's coming back in a few hours to stand watch again."

"Does *everyone* in town but me know what happened?" he asked wearily.

"Like I said, there was nothing you could do, and your family is important."

"Suzanne, let's get something straight. *You* are my family, you and you alone. My sister and her kids are important to me, but you are vital. If anything like this ever happens again, you have to let me know immediately. *I* should be able to decide what I do, not you."

He was hurt; I could hear it in his voice. "I'm sorry. You're right."

"If I'd been attacked, would you have wanted to wait a day to find out?" he asked me.

"I said you were right, Jake. The horse is dead. Dismount."

"Okay. Just don't take any more chances until I get there, all right?"

"Grace and I are going to the store to get some ice cream,

and then we're going to watch a movie," I said, deciding it on the spot.

"That sounds safe enough," Jake said.

"Forgive me?" I asked meekly. I hated having my husband mad at me, especially when it was clearly my fault.

"Yes," he said. "What kind of ice cream are you getting?" It was his way of lightening the mood and letting me know that things were good once again between us.

"I may not be able to decide," I said. "Maybe we'll get a sampler pack."

"Do they make those?"

"Well, not specifically, but what's wrong with getting four or five choices?" I asked with a laugh.

"Nothing that I can think of. Save a little for me."

"I'm not making any promises. Jake, don't speed home. I'm really fine."

"Now I'm the one who isn't going to make any promises. I'll see you soon, okay?"

"I can't wait," I said. "I love you."

"I love you, too."

After we hung up, I stood there on the deck looking into Grace's wooded backyard. It felt good leveling with Jake about what had happened, and I promised myself that I wouldn't keep anything like that from him ever again.

My wrist brushed against the wood of the rail again, missing the nail this time but still stinging a bit. It reminded me of a scrape I'd gotten in my kitchen three months before. The edge of a cutting tool had caught me unexpectedly, leaving a long, thin, angry line that had taken weeks to go away. The dough cutter's long, flexible steel blade had caught me at just the right angle.

In fact, it was the same implement that I'd been searching for in vain in my kitchen earlier.

Had Emma actually moved it, or had something else, something far more sinister, happened to it?

I got my phone out and started searching through the pictures I'd taken of the crime scene. At the moment I wasn't interested in the shots of Simon Reed's body. Instead, I checked out some of the other images I'd taken of the kitchen. It was hard to see until I used my fingers to zoom in to the image so I could get a closer look.

The dough cutter was gone!

I'd blamed Emma for moving it, but I knew that I'd put it back earlier the morning of the murder when I'd last used it, and there was a very limited number of people who had been in my kitchen since I'd shut it down earlier.

In fact, only three people had been there that I knew of: Simon Reed, the killer, and me.

Everything started tumbling into place as I realized that Simon hadn't died as easily as it had first appeared. If the knife wound hadn't been immediately fatal, I could see him whirling around and trying to find something to defend himself with. The dough cutter had been within his reach, and I could visualize him striking out with it in a desperate attempt to defend himself or, at the very least, mark his attacker so we'd know who had murdered him.

I'd seen an angry mark much like mine earlier, and I suddenly had a strong suspicion who the killer was.

Shalimar had had random scratches on her hands, but I believed that they had come from a cat, exactly as she'd explained.

However, Clint Harpold had scratches of his own, but there had been something different about his arm.

There had been a single long wound there as well.

That explained why he'd been wearing long sleeves on such a warm day.

He didn't want anyone to see the evidence of Simon's counterattack, and he couldn't exactly put the dough cutter back on the shelf after Simon was dead. No doubt he was worried about his DNA being on the blade. No, unless I missed my guess, he'd taken it with him and thrown it away in a dumpster somewhere, maybe at Baxter's.

Either way, now I knew where we needed to start looking.

"What's going on? How did he take it?" Grace asked as she joined me on the back porch.

"He's fine," I said. "I know who killed Simon. Now all we have to do is prove it."

"Don't keep me in suspense! Who killed him?"

"Clint Harpold," I said.

That's when I heard a rustling noise coming from the trees.

"Get inside!" I screamed at Grace as I saw Clint bounding toward us with a gun in his hands.

She tried to do as I told her, but before either one of us could escape, Clint was on us.

He pressed the gun into my back, and I could feel the barrel dig into the skin through my thin T-shirt.

"That's a good idea. Let's all go inside," Clint said.

I knew that if we did that, he'd be able to kill us at his leisure. If we stayed where we were, we might at least have a fighting chance.

"Why did you do it, Clint?" I asked him as I touched Grace's arm lightly. I shook my head gingerly, and she caught on right away that we had to resist going inside at any cost.

"Simon had *everything* that I should have had," he said bitterly. "He had Shalimar in the palm of his hand, and he just threw her away as though she didn't matter. Then I saw him make a pass at Emma, and I followed him into the donut shop to confront him about it. He needed to stop acting like a kid and grow up. She deserved someone better."

"Like you?" I asked, and the barrel dug in a little deeper. It was close enough to my bruised shoulder to cause me to wince in pain, something he didn't seem to mind all that much.

"What's *wrong* with me? Shalimar could do a lot worse. Simon laughed at me! He called me a loser, and he made fun of the Lazy Eye, too! He started saying all of these horrible things about my lack of talent, and I couldn't take it anymore. I grabbed a knife from the rack and I stabbed him!"

"He fought back though, didn't he?"

"Yeah. I didn't see the dough cutter coming," Clint admitted. "You spotted that, didn't you? I knew you were getting close, so I had to stop you from figuring out I did it. If you hadn't ducked at the last second, I wouldn't have had to worry about you anymore, either."

"Are you telling me that you killed a man just because he wasn't treating a girl you liked very nicely, a girl that isn't even interested in you? This all came to be because you were jealous of what someone else had?" I asked him incredulously. How much had Clint built it all up in his own mind? Did he really see a scenario where he ended up with his volatile waitress? Was that why he'd hired her? It surely wasn't for her abilities. It was insane on the face of it, but then again, he wasn't being particularly rational at the moment. I'd expected that kind of behavior from Shalimar and Sherry, but not Clint!

"Shalimar is going to love me sooner or later," he said angrily.

"But she kept talking about getting back together with Simon, that it was finally going to happen, and I couldn't let it! Besides, Simon had it coming. He'd been on my back since culinary school, and he got exactly what he deserved. I'm not telling you again to move it. I'm sick of talking about it. Get inside!"

He pushed me with the gun, and Grace started to go in despite my warning.

"Don't do it!" I said loudly.

I'd been talking to Grace, trying to get her to stop and fight, but Clint must have thought I'd meant him.

"Nobody's ever going to tell me what to do again," he said icily.

He started to move the gun in Grace's direction.

It was the moment I'd been waiting for.

As soon as the weapon was out of my back, I shoved myself backward as hard as I could.

The gun fired as Clint went tumbling back over the railing.

Unfortunately, I went right over with him.

CHAPTER 21

A s I was falling, I realized that the gunshot had missed Grace and had pierced the gutter above our heads. She'd have to have that patched before the next rain, but at least she was safe.

For the moment.

It hadn't been that far a fall, just a few feet, but it had managed to knock the gun out of Clint's hand. My shoulder exploded in pain as I landed on him, but I had to ignore it for the moment. I scrambled around to grab the weapon before he could, but Clint rebounded quicker than I thought was possible. As we fought for the gun, I could tell almost immediately that I was losing the fight.

And then Grace joined in.

She must have leapt off the deck the moment we were falling, because a split second later, it was two against one. As Clint and I struggled to get control of the gun, Grace went straight for his throat.

It was an effective technique, and I felt Clint's grip start to slip a little.

It wasn't much, but it was all that I needed.

I got control of the weapon, and Grace let go of the killer's throat.

"Get up," I said as I stood, moving back a few paces in case he tried to lunge out and fight me for the weapon again.

"Make me," Clint said as he lay there in the grass, panting heavily as he tried to get his breath back.

"Do as she says," a strong, familiar voice said from behind me.

It was Chief Grant, but what really caught me off guard was who was with him.

Evidently Theodore Reed had been nearby all along after all.

CHAPTER 22

"WHAT ARE YOU DOING HERE?" I asked him.

"I've been watching out for you since I took off," Theodore said. "I knew that whoever killed my brother wouldn't be able to ignore you for long."

"That was you in front of the shop this morning, wasn't it?" I asked as the chief took the gun from me before handcuffing Clint.

"I didn't want you to see me," he admitted.

"I have a question," Grace said. "Why didn't you help us just now instead of running away?"

"He had a gun!" Theodore said. "I went to get help. What more could I have done?"

"You could have joined the fight," Grace said.

"And risk getting shot? I don't think so," Theodore said, and then he turned to go.

"You're as bad as your brother," Clint said in disgust. I couldn't believe that the killer was taking my side of the argument.

"Whatever," Theodore said as he started to leave again.

"You're just going to let him walk away?" Grace asked the chief incredulously.

"I don't have any choice. He didn't do anything wrong. Besides, he *did* come and get me."

"And left us to face Clint alone," I said.

All the chief could do was shrug. "Let's go, you," Chief Grant said as he pushed the killer toward the street.

"Did you really think you were going to get away with it?" I asked as they walked away.

"If you two meddlesome hags hadn't butted in where you didn't belong, I probably would have," he said, spitting out the words with sheer hate.

"I take that as a compliment," I said.

"You would," he replied.

"I'm so happy you're okay," Jake said as he wrapped his arms around me an hour later at Grace's place. He must have broken, or at the very least bent, the speed limit to get there so quickly, but I was glad that he had. Being in his embrace again, I let the tension leave my body as I nearly collapsed against him. I hadn't even realized how much I'd been holding in until I let it all go.

"Me, too," I said, finally pulling away. "How are things with Paul?"

"It's not important," he said, pulling me in again.

I resisted. "Of course it is. He's family too, Jake."

"Like I said, you're all I really need in the world. We'll deal with the other stuff later. All that matters at the moment is that you're safe."

"As much as I'm enjoying your arms wrapped around me, could you ease up a little?" I asked. "My shoulder's still pretty sore."

"Sorry about that," he said, loosening his grip slightly. "Suzanne, what am I going to do with you?"

"You're going to keep me, I hope," I said with a grin.

"There's no doubt about that. Are you ready to go home?" he asked.

"Could we make one stop along the way?" I asked.

"Sure, but there's nothing between here and our cottage."

"I didn't say that it would be a direct route, but if you don't mind, I'd still like that ice cream."

He laughed heartily. "We'll buy you one of every flavor in stock," he said.

"Don't make promises you aren't willing to keep, sir," I told him with a grin.

"I wouldn't dream of it," he replied.

We didn't buy every flavor they had on hand, but we did manage to put a dent in their inventory. It was a nice evening, and I didn't have to go to bed for at least an hour, so we sat out on our front porch eating ice cream and chatting about nothing, just being together.

The two of us had what Clint Harpold had so desperately wanted, but I couldn't feel sorry for him.

Instead of looking for someone who could love him back, he'd decided to eliminate his main rival, at least in his mind, and the result had been pure and utter chaos.

It was no way to find love, but it was surely a perfect path toward ruin, and I was glad once again that I had Jake in my life.

I loved and was loved in return, I had a job I thrived at and that I was good at, and my family and friends were nearly too many to count.

In every way that mattered, I was the wealthiest woman alive, and I knew it.

And in the end, it was truly the only thing that mattered.

RECIPES

Cherry Cheating Donuts

The reason these are called cheating donuts is because some folks don't think they are donuts at all due to their simplicity to make and the lack of many ingredients. I don't draw that particular line of distinction just because I use a few simple items to prepare them. For me, the true test is in the taste, and trust me, these things are fantastic! In fact, they are better than some of the recipes I make from scratch, but don't tell my family and friends I said that! Fillings are easy enough. Just grab your favorite jam or preserve and you're all set.

This is a fun way to start getting used to making fried goodies, and if they aren't to your liking, all you've lost is a little bread, some filling, a few simple ingredients, and the oil used to fry them in. I'm willing to bet that you'll enjoy them as much as we do though, and a dusting of powdered confectioners' sugar at the end makes the perfect topping.

Ingredients

For the Batter:
- 1 cup all-purpose unbleached flour
- 3⁄4 cup milk (whole or 2%)
- 1 egg

- 2 teaspoons baking powder
- 2 teaspoons granulated sugar
- 1/4 teaspoon salt

Additional Ingredients:
- 4 to 6 slices of bread, any kind you prefer (we use white for this)
- Fruit-based jam or preserves (use your favorite; cherry is our go-to choice)
- Cinnamon sugar or confectioners' sugar
- Canola oil for frying

Directions

Heat enough canola oil to fry your treats to 365 degrees F.

While you're waiting for that to come to temperature, grab a medium mixing bowl and sift the dry ingredients together. Then, in a larger bowl, beat the egg and add the milk. Add the dry mix to the wet, and stir it in well to make a dipping batter.

Next, cut the crusts from the bread and make jam sandwiches with the fruit-based filling of your choice. Cut the sandwiches into four equal pieces, sealing the edges with your fingers, or you can use a ravioli maker to cut out round shapes and seal the edges as well.

Dip each small segment into the batter and then add to the fryer, turning until both sides are golden brown.

Dust with confectioners' sugar or cinnamon sugar, and enjoy!

Makes 8 to 12 treats

Lemon Wow Donuts

I freely admit that I go through phases where I just can't get enough of the cool, refreshing taste of lemon. Summer in particular is my favorite time of year to make these treats. There are several ways of enhancing the lemon taste in a basic cake donut recipe, but I've found over the years that a donut too tart for one person is too mild for the other. This is one of those recipes where experimenting is the order of the day. Don't be afraid to play with the proportions of lemon juice, lemonade, and lemon zest that you use. That's half the fun, in my opinion.

Ingredients

- 1 1/2 cups all-purpose flour
- 1 teaspoon baking soda
- 4 teaspoons confectioners' sugar
- Dash of salt
- 1 egg, beaten
- 1/4 cup milk (whole or 2%)
- 1/4 cup lemonade (sweetened)
- 2 teaspoons lemon juice
- Lemon zest (one lemon)
- Four crushed lemon candies, about 1 tablespoon (entirely optional)
- Canola oil, enough to submerge the donuts

Directions

Heat enough canola oil to fry your treats to 365 degrees F.

While the oil is heating, in a medium-sized bowl, sift the flour, baking soda, confectioners' sugar, and salt together. Set it aside, and in a larger bowl, beat the egg, then add the milk, lemonade, lemon juice, and lemon zest. Stir to combine the ingredients, then slowly add the dry mix to the wet, stirring thoroughly as you go, adding the candy pieces last. Use two tablespoons, one to scoop the batter and the other to slide it off into the oil once it comes to temperature. Cook each drop for 2 to 3 minutes until golden brown, and then remove from the oil and place on a paper towel. A dusting of confectioners' sugar is optional, but we always do it at my house!

Makes approximately 12 lemon drop donuts

Baked Cherry Delights

Sometimes I like to bake my donuts instead of deep-frying them. Not only are they healthier, but the cleanup is quite a bit easier. Baked donuts are surprisingly tasty, and I've converted several of my standard fried donuts to baked versions over the years. You can use your oven, or if you find yourself making more and more baked donuts, you might want to buy an electric donut baker. The rings are already in the equipment, and it works on much the same principle as a countertop waffle maker. These donuts are quite good, and I find that I'm making them quite often by request, something that's always a good sign with my crew!

Ingredients

- 1 egg, beaten slightly
- 1/2 cup milk (whole or 2%)
- 1 tablespoon butter, melted (Contrary to most bakers, I use salted butter.)
- 1/2 cup granulated white sugar
- 2 teaspoons vanilla extract
- 1 cup unbleached all-purpose flour
- 1 teaspoon baking soda
- 1 teaspoon baking powder
- 1/4 teaspoon salt
- 3/4 cup dried fruit (any combination of fruit bits like raisins, cranberries, apples, apricots, or cherries will work just fine)

Directions

Set your oven to 375 degrees F, or turn on your donut maker and let it come to temperature.

While you are waiting, grab a medium mixing bowl and sift the flour, baking soda, baking powder, and salt together. Set aside, and take another bowl, beating the egg first, and then mixing in the milk, melted butter, sugar, and vanilla extract. Slowly add the dry ingredients to the wet mix, stirring until it's all been mixed in well. Don't overmix here, as it might make for tougher treats than you bargain for.

Add the batter to your donut pan for the oven or your maker and bake for 7 to 11 minutes, or until a toothpick comes out cleanly from the donut and it's reached a golden hue.

Remove to a cooling rack, and then coat with a basic sugar glaze (milk, vanilla extract, and confectioners' sugar) or just dust lightly with confectioners' sugar.

Makes 5 to 8 donuts, depending on the pan size.

If you enjoy Jessica Beck Mysteries and you would like to be notified when the next book is being released, please visit our website at jessicabeckmysteries.net for valuable information about Jessica's books, and sign up for her new-releases-only mail blast.

Your email address will not be shared, sold, bartered, traded, broadcast, or disclosed in any way. There will be no spam from us, just a friendly reminder when the latest book is being released, and of course, you can drop out at any time.

OTHER BOOKS BY JESSICA BECK

A Real Pickle
A Burned Biscuit

The Ghost Cat Cozy Mysteries
Ghost Cat: Midnight Paws
Ghost Cat 2: Bid for Midnight

The Cast Iron Cooking Mysteries
Cast Iron Will
Cast Iron Conviction
Cast Iron Alibi
Cast Iron Motive
Cast Iron Suspicion

Made in the USA
San Bernardino, CA
20 April 2019